RESCUE ME

A Heathens Ink Novel
By K.M.Neuhold

CONTENTS

SYNOPSIS

I'll save you as many times as I have to, even if it means saving you from yourself

My heart pounds erratically as the crowd swells around us, panic thick in the air. This can't be how I die, not here, not tonight. Through the throng of bodies, I can see him...*Thane*. Of all the ways I thought tonight would end, this wasn't even on my list. Pain lances through me and I can tell by the look in his eyes that whatever just happened, it's bad. My hand reaches for my leg and I find it sticky and wet with my own blood.

Whatever happens, I know Thane will save me.

Screams, and blood, and tragedy haunt my dreams. I'm alive and I owe it all to the gorgeous former marine who refused to leave me for dead. But how can I start a new relationship when I'm not even sure who I am anymore?

COPYRIGHT

CHAPTER 1

Thane

The thumping bass echoes in my chest as I scan the dance floor, drink in hand. I can't think of a better way to unwind after a long week than finding a gorgeous man to warm my bed. It's been...damn I can't even remember how long it's been since I last had the company of anyone other than my right hand. And, the guys here tonight are all kinds of mouthwatering. It's like a buffet of sexy. How about a little beefcake with a side of twink? *Don't mind if I do.*

I turn my gaze to the bar and my attention snags on a man. I'd like to say he's just like any other man, but something about him immediately draws me in. He leans over the bar and says something to the bartender that causes him to throw his head back and laugh. My eyes travel over my man's — and he *will* be *my man* — tight, round ass and lithe frame. I mentally catalogue the tattoos on both his arms and wonder if he has any more hidden under his clothes.

The bartender slides a drink across the bar and then pulls a pen out of his back pocket and jots something—no doubt his phone number—down on a napkin before pushing that across the bar top as well. *Oh, hell no, this one's mine.*

I gulp down what's left of the beer in my glass and make my way up to the bar, sidling up beside the man who *will* be screaming my name later tonight.

"Let me get that for you," I offer, handing the bartender a ten-dollar bill before the other man can. My man turns his head and looks me up and down. My breath catches as I take in his emerald eyes and dimpled smile. There is no way I'm leaving the club tonight without him.

"Thanks. Madden," he offers his name and an extended hand.

"Thane," I provide mine in return and take his hand, noticing the firm warmth of his grip. I linger on the handshake for a few extra seconds, openly allowing my eyes to roam over his body. Madden does the same to me, and I'm happy to let him look. He seems to be pleased with what he sees because after a few beats he tilts his head toward some booths off to the side of the bar. I'm happy to follow.

"So, *Thane,*" he says my name like it's rich chocolate on his tongue, "what do you do for a living?"

I grin, preparing myself for the response I know I'm about to receive. Telling a man what I do never fails to hit swoon factor ten.

"I'm a fireman."

"Be still my beating heart," he jokes, fanning

himself dramatically.

"So, your place or mine?"

"Pump the breaks, stud. I'm not *that* easy. If you play your cards right we can talk location later." Madden winks at me and sips his drink. His gentle rebuff only gets me hotter for him. It's nice to have a guy who doesn't take much convincing, but it's so much more fun when they make you work for it.

"Fair enough. What do you do, Madden?"

"Tattoo artist," he says. "You've got some decent ink." He reaches out and traces the tribal tat on my left bicep with his index finger.

"Thanks. I'm in the market for more. Where do you work?"

"Heathens Ink. It's not far from here." He reaches into his pocket, pulls out his business card, and hands it to me. Then he notices the Semper Fi tattoo on my right bicep and grins. "Wow, a fireman and a marine. Boys must bend right over to grab their ankles at the snap of your fingers."

"I don't hear the word 'no' a lot," I confirm with a laugh.

"Now I almost feel like I shouldn't let you take me home, just so there's a little balance in the universe."

"Oh, come on now, that would be cruel."

"You're right, that'd be a punishment to both of us. I should warn you, if you're looking for a guy to bend-over I'm not him. I'd be happy to flip you for it though." His voice ends on a low, seductive note that has every nerve ending in my body on fire. *Where has this man been my whole life?*

"Now you're talking my language." The thought of taking turns topping has my insides turning to lava. I don't mind bottoming, but usually I prefer to top. Madden's hard body pressed close to me in the booth, his green eyes boring into mine. I think I could be persuaded to do just about anything for him and beg for more.

"Alright, we're playing a game," Madden announces decisively, waving down the waitress a few feet from our table and orders another drink. "Never have I ever. You start."

"Never have I ever kissed a man."

Madden rolls his eyes at the softball of a first round and we both take a drink.

"Never have I ever punched a shark," Madden declares.

I snort a laugh as Madden takes another drink.

"You have not punched a shark," I argue.

"It was an inflatable pool toy, but I'm pretty sure that still counts."

"Never have I ever had a five-person orgy in a public bathroom," I challenge.

When Madden drinks again I slam my drink down in mock outrage.

"Come on, I know that one's not true."

"Prove it," he challenges with a wink. "Never have I ever, kissed a fireman."

This time he doesn't drink, and the invitation is clear in his green eyes.

Without conscious thought or decision, I find myself leaning in, drawn to him like a moth to a flame. Madden meets me halfway, undeniably as eager as I am to explore the attraction between us. His warm, soft lips mold to mine, sending a jolt of electricity down my spine. I groan in desperation, grabbing the back of his head, deepening the kiss. He tastes like cinnamon and apples and man. He whimpers into my mouth, tangling his tongue with mine.

I pull back a fraction of an inch, Madden's ragged breath bathing my face and short-circuiting my senses.

"God you taste good," I murmur, nipping at his full bottom lip then soothing it with a lick.

"I could say something so dirty right now, but it would be too easy."

I bite back a moan at the mental image he's put in my mind.

"Come home with me."

Madden nods 'yes' and I do a mental fist pump. I pull him back for one more taste, unable to get enough of his intoxicating flavor.

The heart stopping sound of a terrified scream pierces the din of the club. My heart stutters for a second before my training kicks in. Where other's minds fog in panic, mine has been trained to become sharper. Madden's eyebrows draw together in confusion as I stand and attempt to assess where the scream came from. And then a loud pop rings out. *The sound of a gunshot.*

Like a stereo suddenly cranked up to its highest volume, everyone in the club explodes into chaos. Screams echo over the pounding bass of whatever techno song is still blaring through the speakers. More shots ring out, but it's impossible to tell from what direction. I reach for Madden's hand to get him to safety. Once I know he's out of danger I can come back and help whoever else needs it. But the man beside me is my first priority.

People are shoving and panicking, like rats in a trash compactor, frantic to escape with their lives. My hand on Madden's wrist, I pull him in the direction of the exit as the crowd rages around us like the ocean in a storm. I've lost track of how many times I've heard the gun go off, but I'm positive the sound is getting closer to us. Someone shoves hard into Madden, and my grasp on his arm is wretched away.

"Fuck," I mutter, turning to seek out Madden in the mob. I spot him, but it's impossible for me to get to him, the entire crowd pushing forward, and Madden ten feet back from me.

And then another shot penetrates the sound of hysteria, and to my horror Madden goes down. Two more shots in quick succession and my heart is in my throat as I forgo ceremony and start shoving people out of my way to get to him.

My eyes land on Madden who's in a bloody heap on the floor, being trampled with no regard.

I throw myself over him to protect him from the stampede.

"Madden, talk to me." I try to assess his injuries, but in the dark of the club— with nothing but strobing lights—it's impossible to tell where he's bleeding from. As afraid as I am to move him, I'm more afraid to leave him where he is. So, I ease him over my shoulder, eliciting a pained gasp from him. "I've got you, don't worry."

Pushing my way through the crowd is even more difficult now that I have an injured man over my back. I've never been more grateful for my marine training.

When the cool night air hits my face I breathe a momentary sigh of relief. At least now I can check Madden's injuries without being trampled.

The faint sound of sirens in the distance puts me even more at ease. *Help is on the way.*

I guide Madden gently to the ground. His breathing is irregular and he's starting to shiver. *Fuck, he's going into shock.* I notice that his left pant leg is soaked through with blood and his foot is twisted at an odd angle. *Please don't let a bullet have grazed his femoral artery.*

"Stay with me, sweetheart. Help's almost here." I put pressure on his leg in attempt to suppress the bleeding until paramedics can arrive.

People all around us are frantically looking for their friends, terrified of who might have ended up on the wrong end of the gunman.

As fire engines and ambulances barrel into the parking lot some people start to cry out in relief.

"Thane, is that you?" The voice of Hayden, one of my closest friends at work, comes from a few feet away. I look up and try to let him know with my gaze that he needs to get help over here immediately. This wasn't exactly the way I had planned on letting everyone at work know I'm gay, but at this particular moment that's the least of my worries. "Are you hurt?"

"I'm not, but Madden needs immediate attention. I think his femoral artery may have been severed. He's gone into shock."

Hayden nods, a grave expression on his face as he flags down a paramedic and they rush over with a gurney.

"His name is Madden," I tell them as they strap an oxygen mask over his face and carefully load him onto the gurney. "Can I ride with him?"

The paramedic looks at me skeptically. I know it's against the rules unless you're family, but I can't leave Madden's side until I'm sure he's okay. Even then I'm not sure I'll be able to walk away.

"He's one of us," Hayden tells the paramedic in an authoritative tone. The paramedic nods and allows me to follow as they load him into the ambulance.

I reach for Madden's hand as soon as we're in and stay as out of the way as possible as the EMT appraises his injuries and begins his attempt to stabilize him.

"Patient has what appears to be three gunshot wounds, one to the left femoral, possibly severing the artery, one to the abdomen with excessive bleeding as well. And the third to the right forearm. He's going to need a transfusion," the EMT radio's in.

"I'm O negative, universal donor, I'll give blood," I volunteer without hesitation.

He eyes me warily.

"Sorry man, it's against the law for homosexuals to donate blood."

"Are you fucking kidding me?" *How did I not know that?* "Do you know how many people may need blood transfusions coming from the club? What if there isn't enough?"

The EMT shrugs and gives me a sympathetic look.

"Rules are rules. We're going to do everything we can for your boyfriend."

I nod, not correcting the 'boyfriend' part. Even if I am a fireman, it's unlikely they'll let me stay with Madden if they find out I've known him an hour.

I'm not a religious man, but I send a prayer out to the universe anyway. Hoping like hell there's someone or something out there with the power to keep Madden alive.

The hospital is a mad house. Doctors and nurses are scrambling to tend to all the shooting victims being brought in. The second we were through the doors I was told to stay in the waiting room as Madden was rushed through a set of doors marked 'no admittance beyond this point'.

I pace the waiting area like a caged lion, muscles coiled ready to pounce on the first medical professional I spot to demand answers. It's been four fucking hours. Madden has to be okay, right? How would I even know? I'm no one. They won't tell me if he's resting peacefully, in critical condition, or...I can't even bare to think the other possibility.

A young, male nurse appears at the triage desk and I'm on him like white on rice.

"I need to know the status of a patient," I demand. He looks rather affronted at my brisk tone and then purses his lips.

"What's your relation to the patient?"

"He's my...husband," I blurt out the lie and then realize I'm going to be totally fucked if he asks any follow up questions, like Madden's last name.

The nurse eyes me up, clearly suspicious.

"Name of patient?" he asks after several tense seconds.

"Madden. He was brought in from the night

club shooting."

"Last name?" He asks.

Fuck.

"Okay, here's the thing…"

"I want to help you, but rules are rules," The nurse says, giving me a sympathetic look. *I swear to god, if one more person says 'rules are rules'…*

"I get that, I do, but I don't even know how to get ahold of his family or anything. I don't want him to wake up alone. Please."

He pulls his bottom lip between his teeth and glances around, like he's making sure he's not about to get caught.

"I shouldn't," he mutters seemingly to himself.

"I'm a firefighter, if I get in trouble, I'll show them my ID and I won't tell them you let me in."

His shoulders sag in defeat.

"He's in room 210, follow me." He tilts his head and I hurry to follow. "He's not awake from surgery yet, but he's no longer critical. Doctor Grant will likely be by tomorrow to discuss everything, and myself or other nurses will be checking in throughout the night. If I get fired for this, there *will* be hell to pay."

"Got it," I assure him with a chuckle. "Thanks so much."

He places a comforting hand on my shoulder and then points at the door in front of me and turns to leave me.

I take a deep breath, steeling myself for whatever condition I'm going to find Madden in. I've seen a lot of shit in my time, but the idea of seeing my beautiful stranger looking broken and battered has my skin crawling. *He's not critical; he's going to be fine.* I chant this reminder in my head for several seconds before I get up the courage to push open the door.

The lights are dimmed in the room and both beds contain sleeping forms. The bed closest to the window contains an older lady, but the person in the bed closer to the door is who I'm looking for.

Madden looks pale but peaceful. The machines attached to him beep out a steady, soothing rhythm. I grab the chair that's shoved into a corner and pull it up to Madden's bedside. I place my hand over his and manage to take a full breath for the first time since the initial shot rang out in the club.

"Some night, huh?" I joke to the beautiful, unconscious man before me.

CHAPTER 2

Thane

"With fifteen dead and at least two dozen injured, and less than a year after the Pulse nightclub shooting, the LGBT community is wondering if they'll ever feel safe going to a nightclub again."

"Would you mind turning that off?" I request of the person in the bed beside Madden. The middle-aged woman in the bed gives me a harsh look but flips the channel anyway.

I turn my attention back to Madden's sleeping form. After several hours in surgery and two blood transfusions the nurses tell me he's out of the woods. Still, he hasn't woken up.

About an hour after the nurse let me in to sit with Madden last night, I got a call from my chief who told me Hayden had gotten ahold of him and let him know I was present at the shooting and someone important to me was injured. He told me to take a few weeks off on short term disability so I can be with Madden and to give me time to cope with being involved in a mass shooting.

Madden's cell phone- retrieved from his tattered, bloody pants- buzzes on the bedside table. I consider ignoring it, but it may be someone worried they haven't been able to get ahold of him. I grab the phone and find several texts from a man named Adam, starting from yesterday around the time the news picked up the story of the shooting.

> **Adam:** Dude, just saw the news, fucked up.
>
> **Adam:** Royal just called me. He's freaked because he says you were going to the club last night. CALL ME
>
> **Adam:** Seriously, you're making me nervous. Call me
>
> **Adam:** There's a picture on FB that looks like you, being carried out of the club. Please tell me it wasn't you. Please, man. Please call me.

My stomach twists as I read through the frantic texts. I don't know who this man is, but it's obvious he cares about Madden. I type out a quick text from Madden's phone in response.

> **Madden:** Hi, I'm a friend of Madden's. He's in the hospital, I'm here with him. He's stable, but unconscious still.
>
> **Adam:** Holy fuck. Ok, thanks for letting me know. I'll be there soon.

I let out a long breath and glance back over at the unconscious man before me. Every time I page a nurse to ask if he should've woken up by now, they keep telling me he's stable and will wake up when the drugs wear off and his body is ready.

His phone chirps in my hand with a Facebook notification. I shouldn't snoop, but I'm curious about the man who nearly died in my arms. The only thing I know about him is his name and he kisses like a fucking god. I'd kill to know everything.

Without even trying to talk myself out of it, I click on the Facebook icon on his home screen and start to scroll through his page, desperate to know more about him.

His profile picture is a selfie of himself and three guys in front of a sign that says, 'Heathens Ink'. I remember he mentioned that's the name of the shop he tattoos at. He has a temporary border around the image that says 'No H8' in rainbow colors. My lips twitch in a sad smile. *If only*.

I click through more of his pictures to find many more of him with those same four guys and one woman. There are a ton of pictures of tattoos or of him tattooing his friends from the other pictures. To my relief there are no definitive 'couple' pictures of him kissing any guys. After I've looked through the pictures, I click on the groups he follows to get a better idea of what he's into. Predictably, he belongs to a number of tattoo groups and LGBTQ groups. His likes include a lot of books I've never heard of, and some I have. I'm just about to start snooping on his friends list when I'm interrupted. I set the phone back on the nightstand before his friends notice I was snooping. Although, they're too focused on Madden to have noticed anyway.

"Madden, holy fuck." A man with a bushy beard and tattoos covering almost every inch of exposed skin, bursts into the hospital room in a state of dismay, two other men and a woman behind him, all looking equally distressed. I recognize them all from the pictures on his Facebook and assume one of them is Adam.

"Shh, he's resting," I chide protectively. I'm sure they've got Madden on more than enough drugs to sleep through just about anything, but I don't want to take the risk.

"Oh my god, you're the guy," the bearded man says. "You saved him." He rushes forward and wraps me in a hug, nearly toppling the shitty plastic chair they gave me to sit in.

"I'm Thane," I offer once he lets go of me. "How'd you know what happened?"

"Dude, there are pictures of you carrying him out of the club, all over the news and internet. I'm Adam by the way, Madden's friend and roommate."

Adam introduces me to Gage, their other roommate, who is also covered in tattoos but has short, blue hair, and no beard. Royal, who is a few inches shorter than the other two men, with his hair buzzed on the sides and long on top, again covered in tattoos. Nash, who's tall and built, with long dark hair pulled up into a man-bun. And finally, Dani, a sprite of a woman who seems like she can hold her own with all these men.

"I should've been there with him," Royal laments, sinking down at the foot of the bed and placing a hand on Madden's calf. His eyes glisten with unshed tears as he looks at the beautiful, broken man I've only just met. I bristle inwardly. *Is this man something more to Madden than a friend?*

"Me too," Gage mutters, with a far-off look in his eyes.

"Then you'd both be in the hospital bed beside him," Adam argues with them both. "I guarantee if Madden had any time to be glad of anything, he was glad he didn't put you in danger as well."

"Still, I should've been there." Royal says again.

"How do you know, Madden, by the way?" Gage asks me after a few moments of silence as all of Madden's friends stood looking over him, no doubt hoping he'll be okay.

"We met at the club, actually."

"Oh jeez. Well, you look exhausted. I'm sure he appreciates everything, but we're here now so you can go if you need to," Adam offers.

"No, I'm not going anywhere until he wakes up."

Adam nods and everyone lapses into silence, the only sound is the faint beep, beep, beep of the machines monitoring Madden's vitals, and the snoring of the old lady in the other bed.

The sound of rustling pulls me from an uncomfortable sleep. There's a crick in my neck from dozing on the hospital provided chair, and my ass is completely numb. But I smile none-the-less because I'm looking into the most beautiful emerald eyes I've ever seen.

His gaze is a bit unfocused and confused, but he's awake and I couldn't be happier.

"Are you a nurse? And if so, can I get my sponge bath now?" His sleepy, husky tone does all kinds of delicious things to my insides. And his flirtatious comment is a balm on my soul.

"I'm not a nurse, but I think we can arrange something," I tease, sitting forward in the chair and taking his hand in mine. His fingers give mine a feeble squeeze.

"What happened?"

"Some asshole decided to shoot up the club. Tried to make you into Swiss cheese, sweetheart."

Madden winces but then lets out a rough laugh.

"I feel more like American cheese right now, all sticky and gross."

"Do you want some water or something?"

Madden nods and attempts to sit up. I rush forward to steady him and help him into a sitting position. His hospital gown falls off one shoulder, revealing more colorful ink I hadn't had the chance to see before.

Once he's sitting, I offer him a Styrofoam cup filled with water, and a little straw to make it easier for him to drink.

"Do you need anything else?"

A blush creeps into his cheeks as he looks at me and then looks past me toward the small bathroom in the corner of the room.

"Ah, maybe we should page the real nurse for that one." I grab the call button off the bedside table and press it before taking his hand again. For some reason, everything in the universe feels right when I'm touching him. *I don't even know his last name.*

"What are you still doing here?"

He asks at the same time I say, "What's your last name?"

We both chuckle and I wave for him to answer first.

"Brody. It's written right up there," Madden says, gesturing to the giant white board on the wall opposite the foot of his bed listing his name and times his medications and vital checks are due.

"I can't believe I didn't notice that. I've been obsessing about your last name for two days," I lament. "*Madden Brody,* I like it. My last name is Grayson, by the way."

"Not that I'm not grateful, Thane Grayson, but why are you still here? You look like you haven't slept in a week."

"Nah, just two days. I can leave if you want," I offer reluctantly.

"No." His grasp on my fingers tightens and the cold fingers of disappointment around my heart ease. Maybe he's feeling this crazy need to be near each other like I am. I don't believe in love at first sight, but I do believe in gut feelings.

The nurse peaks her head in and beams at Madden.

"Well, well, well look who's awake. How are you feeling?"

"Like I've been shot a few times," Madden deadpans. "And, like I really need to use the bathroom."

She nods in understanding before offering him a bedside urinal.

"Sorry, but I can't let you out of bed just yet until the doctor has a chance to assess your leg again."

Madden grimaces.

"How about if I go down to the cafeteria and grab you something to eat?" I offer to give him a chance for privacy. "Wait, is he allowed to eat?" I ask the nurse.

"He can eat. The surgery itself was mild. It was just a laparoscopic procedure on his abdomen. There might be nausea from the medications though, so take it easy."

I nod and turn to head for the door.

"Thane," Madden calls out. I stop and turn back to face him. "Thanks for...everything."

"You don't have to thank me," I assure him before turning again and heading out in search of food.

Madden

If there's anything more awkward than pissing in a hand-held urinal I have yet to find out what it is. I'm glad the sexy fireman who kisses like a god and saved my life, spared my dignity and stepped out for a few minutes. I don't quite understand what he's doing here, waiting at my bedside, but I'm not about to question it.

My brain is still foggy, not conjuring the events clearly. What I do remember is making out with Thane, chaos as we tried to leave the club, pain, and looking into his soulful brown eyes as he told me everything was going to be okay.

My heart starts to thunder and the beeping of the heart monitor speeds up, as sensory memories of that night flash through my mind. There was so much screaming. The reverberating pop, pop, pop of the gun being fired. I lean forward in the bed, burying my face in my hands as I try to breathe.

"Hey, whoa, what's the matter sweetheart? Talk to me." I didn't notice Thane coming back into the room, but his hands are on my back, rubbing in calming circles, and his voice is authoritative yet soothing. He's in fireman mode.

"I was thinking about what happened," I gasp out between painful breaths. My heart is still hammering, forcing me to take deep, dragging breaths which are setting my stomach on fire.

"You need to try taking slower breaths. You're going to hurt yourself if you don't calm down. Now, take a deep breath in, and hold it."

I do as he instructs, filling my lungs and holding it. He starts to slowly count to ten and then he tells me to let the breath out.

We repeat the process until the heart monitor returns to normal.

"You had a panic attack. Are you feeling okay now?"

I nod and duck my head in embarrassment. The last thing I wanted was for the sexy fireman/marine to think I'm a total pansy.

Thane gently tilts my chin up so I'm looking at him and he gives me a reassuring smile.

"It's completely normal under the circumstances. Now, why don't we have something to eat and then you can get some more rest."

I nod and he offers me a pre-made turkey sandwich.

"Sorry, it's not very exciting. It's two in the morning, so the only thing you can get down there right now is pre-packaged stuff."

"It's okay. Thank you."

We make small talk while we eat. Thane tells me about meeting my friends and roommates and how Royal seemed to feel guilty for not coming to the club with me. When Thane mentions Royal, there's a flash of something in his eyes that almost seems like jealousy.

"So, have you and Royal been friends long?"
Bingo, it is jealousy.

"A few years," I give a vague answer so I can watch him squirm for a second.

"Huh. And I'm assuming he's gay, since you invited him to the club?" Thane picks at his sandwich, sneaking glances at me to gauge my answers.

"Bisexual, actually."

"Huh."

Guess I'd better put the poor guy out of his misery.

"He's got a hopeless crush on his straight best friend, poor guy. He probably came by too. Nash?"

"Yep, he was here."

Thane breaths out a sigh of relief. It feels kind of nice to have someone jealous over me. My most recent ex-boyfriend was never jealous. Turned out it was because he was too busy fucking other guys to worry about what I was doing. I bet Thane would never cheat. He seems like a great boyfriend. Not that I'm thinking about him *that* way. We just met, after all. There's potential there, though. Maybe.

My eyelids start to feel heavy and the pillow beckons my head.

"Let me help you lay back down," Thane offers, and his firm but gentle hands guide me with as little jostling as possible. "Sleep well, sweetheart." His lips brush my forehead just before I drift off to sleep.

Thane

"That cannot be comfortable."

I'm startled awake by the murmurs of Madden's friends.

"How badly does your neck hurt right now?" Adam asks, eyeing my awkward sleeping position.

"On a scale of one to ten? About a twelve."

"Can't a gunshot victim get a little shut eye around here?" Madden mutters from his bed. Adam jumps back, startled while Dani squeals with excitement.

"Oh my god, how are you feeling?" She asks sitting on the edge of the bed and taking Madden's hand. He gives her fingers a little squeeze and then opens his eyes.

"I'll be alright, babe. It'll take more than a few bullets to stop the Mad Dog."

"So, what's the prognosis, man?" Gage asks, stepping forward and touching Madden's leg, like he needs to assure himself his friend is really there and okay.

"Haven't seen the doctor yet. But, I'm pretty sure I'll live," Madden deadpans.

"Madden, listen," Royal bites the lip ring through the left side of his bottom lip and turns a sorrowful gaze on his friend.

"Royal, dude, don't even try to apologize for not being there. If I'm thankful for anything, it's that you weren't there to risk getting hurt or worse."

"Told you," Adam crows.

The doctor chooses that moment to enter the room.

"Looks like your friends found you," the doctor says with a jovial smile. "I'm Doctor Grant. Can I kick your friends out for a few minutes so we can chat?"

"Can they stay?"

"If you're comfortable with me discussing your condition with them here," Doctor Grant agrees. "You were in pretty rough shape when you were brought in. I'm not going to sugar coat it for you, it was a close call. One bullet did some muscle damage to your right forearm. You might have limited use as far as fine motor skills for the foreseeable future and may never regain full use."

Madden gasps and flexes the fingers. He winces and then turns a concerned gaze in Adam's direction. It doesn't take a genius to realize he's worried about what this means for his tattoo career.

"The second bullet passed through your abdomen and lodged in a rib. We did surgery to remove it. Luckily, there was no extensive damage caused. You'll be sore for a little while, and will need to take it easy."

Madden nods, seeming less concerned about this news than the previous.

"The final bullet passed through your left

thigh, nicking your femoral artery. That was where you lost the majority of blood and why the transfusions were necessary. That was repaired surgically. You'll notice tenderness and bruising, but otherwise I expect that will heal without incident. Finally, your right ankle sustained a transverse fracture, I'm assuming by the stampeding crowd. I've placed pins to stabilize the bones. You won't be able to bear weight for six to eight weeks on that leg."

Madden lets out a long breath as he takes in all of the information the doctor dumped on him.

"I live in a five-floor walk-up," Madden murmurs, looking again at Adam. The doctor frowns.

"Is there anywhere else you could stay for a while? There's no way you'll be able to do five flights of stairs on a consistent basis, not for six weeks, at least."

"Fuck," Madden lays his head back on his pillow and closes his eyes. "I guess I could try to find a different apartment, I've got some money saved."

"There isn't any family you could stay with?" Doctor Grant asks.

"No," Madden's answer is terse, making me curious about his family situation. That's a question for a different day.

"You can stay with me. I've got a house with a guest bedroom on the first floor. No stairs required," I blurt before I can think better of it.

"You don't have to do that," Madden argues.

"I'll let you talk this out. I'm going to plan

to have you discharged in about an hour." Doctor Grant gives Madden a friendly smile before excusing himself.

"I know I don't *have* to sweetheart. I have extra space and I don't mind."

"We don't even know each other."

"He *did* save your life," Adam points out.

"So, you think I should go stay with him?" Madden asks Adam. The vulnerability in Madden's tone and the way he looks to Adam like he'll trust whatever his decision is, makes me wonder about the dynamic of their relationship.

"I think it's the best option at the moment. A five-floor walk-up isn't going to work, Royal and Nash don't have extra space, Dani lives with her mom, and you shouldn't be living alone when you are healing from such a major event," Adam reasons.

"Alright," Madden nods in agreement and turns back to me. "Thank you for offering. I can't understand why you're doing so much for me when I'm a complete stranger but *thank you*."

"It's not a problem," I assure him. "Now stop thanking me."

"Not a chance," Madden says with a smile.

CHAPTER 3

Thane

Adam was nice enough to run home and gather up as many of Madden's clothes and essentials as possible and is bringing them back for him.

Madden had been extremely quiet since the doctor had stopped in, and everyone seems afraid to ask him how he's feeling. His friends make small talk about the tattoo shop they all work at; the same one Madden gave me the business card to when we met two nights ago. *Jesus, that seems like it was a different lifetime.*

Am I completely insane for inviting a stranger to come live with me for an undetermined length of time?

I glance over at Madden, looking fragile but infinitely more vital than he did when I pulled him out of the club. My heart flutters and my skin prickles with the need to protect him, care for him, and make sure he's whole and well. It doesn't make any sense; I don't even know this guy. *But I want to know him.*

Madden shifts in the hospital bed and his features pinch with discomfort.

"When were your last pain meds? You're

probably due." I reach for the call button to page the nurse, but Madden puts his hand on mine to stop me.

"I'll be alright. It's not so bad."

I bite my tongue against arguing with him. He's an adult and he can choose not to take his pain medication if he wants.

"You guys are going to have to call my appointments scheduled over the next few months and either take them yourselves or reschedule until my arm is back in working order."

"Of course. We'll take care of everything, you don't need to worry," Gage assures him. Still, Madden worries his bottom lip as he turns his attention back to the television and stares blankly ahead.

Madden

When I was a kid my grandma used to say your whole life can change in a fraction of a second, no warning necessary. This is the third time I've lived the truth of that statement. The first was when my parents found out I was gay at fourteen and kicked me out. The second was when Adam was willing to take a chance on a homeless, junkie for a tattoo apprenticeship based solely on my sketch book. The third was the moment the doctor told me I may never have full use of my right hand again. No more tattooing, no more art. Who am I without my art? I was an addict and a loser before I was a tattoo artist. *So, who am I now?*

The sweet blonde nurse from earlier enters the room with a stack of papers and a smile.

"I bet you're itching to get out of here, so let me go over your discharge paperwork super quick and we'll get you home to your big, hunky fireman." She winks at Thane to punctuate her statement and he blushes crimson but doesn't correct her that he isn't *my* fireman.

"Thank you," I nod and attempt to sit up. A sharp pain spikes through my abdomen and I fall back with a gasp.

Thane is at my side in an instant, helping me sit up with care. I grit my teeth against the throb in my leg and my abdomen. I don't want Thane, or anyone else, to push the pain med issue. I'm not crazy about the fact that they had me on opioids while I've been here. What if I can't resist taking more when these wear off?

"Okay sweetie," the nurse sits beside me on the bed and hands me the first piece of paper she's holding. "Here's your script for Oxycodone, and another for antibiotics to prevent an infection while you heal."

I stare at the scribbled words, a free pass to a two-week supply of the good stuff. The stuff I used to go into free clinics and fake migraines and injuries, or even steal to get. Even then, it was hard to find doctors willing to give it out. I swallow hard and ball my left hand in a fist in an attempt to control the shaking. I can feel Adam's eyes boring into me. Is he worried I'll backslide? He should be worried, I'm fucking worried.

I want to thrust the prescription back at the nurse, tell her I can't take it with me. It's too much of a temptation. Surely if I tell her I'm an addict she'll take it back and offer me extra strength Tylenol instead. I can't seem to form the words to admit my weakness. Instead, I nod wordlessly and listen as she goes over instructions for my follow-up appointments and exercise restrictions. I feel a blush creep into my cheeks when she glances at Thane and then tells me no sex for a week.

Once she's done going over everything, I'm free to go.

Adam offers me a t-shirt and sweatpants from my suitcase. As I look at the proffered clothes I feel physically exhausted at the thought of trying to get dressed. Thane's gaze bores into me, studying me, and then he turns to my friends with an authoritative stance.

"Why don't you guys say goodbye to Madden and I'll take it from here."

Adam glances my way for approval and I give him a nod.

"Call us if you need *anything.*"

Dani, Royal, Nash and Gage repeat the sentiment and offer gentle hugs before they all depart, leaving me alone with Thane.

"Alright, now let's get you dressed."

"I can do it myself," I argue feebly.

"I know you can, but it'll make me feel better if you let me help."

I shoot Thane a look that says *I see through your bullshit* but allow him to help me. As much as I don't want to need help, I do.

I take a deep breath and hold it as I ease off the bed, keeping the majority of my weight on my left leg. Thane steps forward and I instinctively reach for his broad shoulders to steady myself.

I'm not a small guy by any means, being five eleven and about a hundred and eighty pounds. I've got nothing on Thane. Even in my injured state a small shiver of desire rolls through me at the thought of being pinned beneath his powerful body.

"Are you okay? You're looking flushed. Are you lightheaded or anything?" Thane asks, brushing my disheveled, dirty hair off my forehead and gazing into my eyes.

"I'm alright." I steady myself against him and maneuver into my pants, luckily managing to conceal my junk from Thane's view under my hospital gown. I'm not sure where things will eventually go with him, but I'd rather the first time he sees me naked be a little different than *this.*

Once my pants are on, I shed the gown and enjoy the feeling of Thane's eyes roaming over my chest and arms. I glance down to see the significant bruising and the reddened area the doctor had to sew back together. I wince and immediately look away. Guess the sexy fireman wasn't checking me out after all. More like assessing my injuries.

I grit my teeth against another wave of pain as I lift my arms to slip my shirt over my head. Thane's hands are a gentle pressure on my hips, keeping me steady.

By the time I'm dressed I'm winded and completely spent.

"Fuck, why was it that hard to get dressed?" I complain.

"Because your body is trying to heal and that takes a lot of energy all by itself." Thane runs his fingers along my jaw and brushes a fleeting kiss across my forehead before taking my hand and leading me to the wheelchair the nurse left for me to get downstairs.

I tell my stupid heart to stop fluttering in my chest. I'm sure Thane's being nice to me because I almost died.

Thane

After getting Madden settled into the passenger seat of my SUV– his belongings that Adam brought for him in the backseat— I make my way around to the driver side and jump in.

The awkwardness of being strangers settles over us for the first time as we find ourselves at a loss for words.

"So, uh, where do you live?" Madden asks and then lets out a small laugh. "Guess I should've asked that when you first offered."

"Not far, I've got a small house in Newcastle. Bought it a few years ago once I knew I was going to stay around Seattle."

Madden nods and we lapse into another silence.

"So, firemen work like forty-eight hours straight, right?"

"Twenty-four hours on, then forty-eight hours off. They gave me a few weeks off on FMLA to get my head on straight after everything. Once I go back, you should have one of your friends come stay at my place during my shifts so you aren't without help."

Again, Madden nods, his gaze fixed on the scenery speeding past.

"How'd your family react to your coming out?" He asks after a few minutes.

"I...uh...haven't," I admit, bracing for the closet shaming I usually get when another gay man learns I'm too chicken shit to be 'out'.

Madden shifts in his seat, and I feel his concerned gaze fixed on me.

"Um, Thane, have you been on social media in the past few days?" He asks, his tone cautious.

"No, I'm not much for social media."

"Okay, don't freak out, but I have to show you something." Madden pulls out his phone and starts tapping the screen. As I roll to a stop at a red light, he passes me his phone. I glance at the screen with curiosity and what I see makes my heart leap into my throat and my stomach clench.

"What is this?" It's a stupid question because it's without a doubt me carrying Madden out of the night club over my shoulder, followed by a picture of me gazing down at his prone body with concern and fear.

"It's all over Facebook and Twitter. People are kind of saying things like 'this is what true love looks like'. So... there's a good chance your family is going to see it."

I wait for the dread to wash over me. To my surprise instead of horror at the idea of my family finding out I feel...relief.

I hand him his phone back as the light turns green and I spare a quick, reassuring glance in Madden's direction.

"Not exactly how I planned to tell them, but it's long overdue anyway."

"Really?"

"Yeah, it'll be fine."

Madden

It's not long before we pull into the driveway of a cute two-story colonial house with a well-kept lawn.

"Here we are. Home sweet home."

"I have to thank you again. I know you said not to, but I can't get over how generous it is to let a complete stranger stay in your house indefinitely."

"It's not a problem," Thane assures me again. "Truth be told, it'll be nice having someone else around. It gets sort of creepy quiet when I'm here by myself."

He shuts off the car and hurries around to help me out. My face flames as Thane's arms wrap around my waist to help me stand. It's a bitch to be this helpless. I clench my jaw against the pain as he helps me hobble to the door.

"I've got a crutch you can use, I'll have to dig it out of my closet," Thane says as we reach the door.

With an arm around my waist he digs in his pocket for his keys to open the door. There's a small step up into the house from the porch, during which Thane supports ninety percent of my weight, causing my body temperature to shoot through the roof at the contact.

Thane tosses his keys on a small table right next to the door and then toes off his shoes.

"So, your room is right through there." He points to a room right off the front hallway. "The sheets are fresh. I keep it clean and ready in case my mom ever stops by for a visit unannounced," he explains with a put-upon fondness. That must be nice, having parents who love you. My parents were the other kind, the kind that kick their four-teen-year-old son out on the streets with nowhere to go because they caught him kissing another boy.

"Thanks," I say again, because I can't stop appreciating all the things this near stranger has done for me.

"It's no problem. Are you hungry?"

"I'd kill for a shower."

"Okay. Do you, uh, need help?" His expression is part nervous, part hopeful and makes me hot all over.

"Probably...I'm not sure how I'll...um...get my pants off," I admit, a blush creeping up my neck and over my face. Again, *so* not the way I wanted Thane to see me naked for the first time.

Thane nods— a pink tinge coloring his cheeks as well—before leading me down the short hallway to the bathroom.

He eases me down to sit on the side of the tub while he grabs a towel for me. I take the opportunity to pull my shirt over my head and toss it on the floor. Then, Thane helps me stand again and I try to hide the wince of pain. The last thing I want is for him to push me on the painkiller issue. I may not be able to say no again.

Thane reaches for the waist of my sweatpants and my dick starts to stand up and take notice. Fuck, I thought the pain would be a mood killer, but evidently not.

"I can do that part."

"Oh, right, sorry."

I use my good hand to shove my pants down, leaning my weight against Thane for balance. I do my best to cover my semi, and Thane is enough of a gentleman not to look.

Once I'm stable, he leans into the shower and turns it on, keeping his hand under the water to test the temperature.

"Alright, you should be good to go? Or do

you need me to stay and help?"

"I think I'm okay from here but I'll need help to get out."

He nods as he draws the curtain back and then lifts me up and places me in the shower, keeping a firm grasp on my hips until he's sure I've steadied myself on my good leg.

"Thanks," I say in an embarrassing, breathless tone. I can't help if his hands on me give me very naughty ideas.

"I'll leave the door open so you can yell when you need help again."

I nod and he pulls the curtain back into place, leaving me alone with my dick at half-mast and glorious, hot water soothing my aching muscles.

Thane

As soon as I leave Madden alone to shower, I find myself standing in my living room doing everything in my power to talk my erection into submission. Even with his skin marred with bruises and angry red marks, Madden is still the most attractive man I've ever laid eyes on. The last thing I'm about to do is make things awkward between us. What he really needs is someone to take care of him.

Once I convince my dick we're not doing anything fun with the gorgeous, naked man in the other room, I busy myself checking the guest bedroom to make sure everything is in order and extra bedding is handy. Then, I head to the kitchen and put a frozen pizza in the oven, figuring Madden must be hungry.

Before long, the sound of the shower cuts off and I hear Madden calling my name. My pulse spikes knowing I'm about to have my hands all over his wet body as I help him out of the shower. *And, the erection is back.*

I do a quick adjustment so it's less obvious, because there's no way I'm convincing it to go away again when I know I'm about to be touching him. Then, I head down the hall to the bathroom.

Grabbing the towel off the sink—where I left it before his shower— I hold it out to Madden, studiously not looking at his ripped chest, covered in dark ink.

"Thanks," he mutters, toweling off and wrapping it around his hips.

It's low slung, drawing attention to his v-cut muscles, begging to be licked. *Stop perving on him.* I command myself sternly.

Once he's covered, I step forward and put an arm around his waist, steadying him so he doesn't have to put any weight on his bad leg as he climbs over the lip of the tub to exit the shower. I wait as he pulls his pajama pants on, followed by his t-shirt. I breathe a small sigh of relief once his body is hidden from my lecherous gaze.

"Hungry? I've got a pizza in."

"Starving."

I pass Madden his crutch that I left leaning

against the bathroom door and lead him to the kitchen.

"Your house is nice."

"Thanks. I bought it a few years ago. Felt like settling in, I guess, once I was stable at the station. Apartment living can get kind of old, you know?"

"Tell me about it." Madden nods in agreement. "I've been living with Adam for four years now, and before that..." he clears his throat and shifts in his seat, clearly having almost said something he didn't intend to. "It seems nice to have your own place. Not that I don't like living with Adam and Gage..."

"Yeah, I get it," I agree with a laugh, thinking back to what it was like to have a roommate. Or, worse yet, a whole bunch of roommates when I was in the marines.

"I make enough money to get my own place, but I guess I haven't worked up the balls to tell Adam I'm thinking of moving out."

"He seems like a good guy, I'm sure he'd understand."

Madden nods in agreement. The conversation trails off as I pull the pizza from the oven and we both devour it like we haven't eaten in weeks.

CHAPTER 4

Madden

Every time I close my eyes I'm transported back there. Screams of terror. People shoving, desperate to escape with their lives. The pain slicing through my abdomen. I was positive I was going to die. If not from the bullets, there was no doubt I would've been trampled to death within seconds had Thane not been there. It's not a feeling that's easy to forget.

I can't even toss and turn properly thanks to my injuries. With an irritated sigh I reach for the crutch Thane gave me and, with great effort, manage to get myself out of bed.

By the time I hobble to the couch I'm winded and my abdomen is throbbing, not to mention my leg. I'm glad my pain meds are all the way back in my bedroom, because I'm tempted to take a few. I have a legitimate need this time, that's not the same as being a junkie. I'm sure I could take one when I *really* need it and not fall back into old habits, right?

Biting my lip hard enough to draw blood, I force myself to derail that dangerous train of thought and reach for the remote control for the television.

I've gone four fucking years without touching a pill. The crawling itch under my skin is an unfriendly reminder that I'll always be a drug addict. Even if I go a hundred years without touching that shit, I'll still be a drug addict.

I find a *Golden Girls* marathon and ease myself into a laying position, letting the canned laughter chase away the dark specters in my mind.

I'm somewhere between waking and sleeping when Thane stumbles into the living room in a drowsy haze. His dark hair is sticking up every which way and there's a sexy stubble covering his jaw. My eyes roam over his bare torso, all cut lines and a dusting of dark hair covering his pecs and tapering down the middle of his abs. My cock grows painfully hard in my thin pajama pants, and I stealthily ease a pillow in front of myself to hide it.

Luckily, Thane seems to be in too much of a sleep stupor to realize the middle school move I just pulled to hide my boner.

"You been up long?" he asks in a raspy voice.

I glance up and realize the sun is up.

"What time is it?" I rub my eyes and try to orient my foggy brain.

"Seven."

"Shit," I mutter, running my hands through my hair and then wiping them down my face. "I don't think I slept at all."

Thane's brow furrows with concern.

"Are you okay? Are you in pain? I can grab your meds for you."

"No," I snap, in a harsher tone than intended. "Sorry, I mean, no, I'm fine."

"Alright," Thane's tone holds skepticism, but he doesn't push the issue. "You drink coffee?"

"God yes, a bucket full please."

"One bucket of coffee, coming right up," he calls back as he makes his way to the kitchen.

I rub my hands vigorously over my eyes in an attempt to clear away the cobwebs from my brain.

My eyes are heavy, and every part of my body is aching. I want to call out to Thane that I changed my mind about the pain meds, ask him to bring me some. It's so tempting. Oxy always made me feel like I was wrapped in a warm blanket made of happy. I need some fucking happy right now. Would it be so bad to take one or two?

No. No. No. I will not take any Oxy. I will not fall back into old habits. I am strong.

Thane

While the coffee brews I decide to also scramble up a few eggs for us. I'm dying to ask Madden why he is so insistent on not taking his pain meds, but I think I can guess the answer. There aren't a whole lot of reasons a person is so against taking drugs. The main one being that they *really* like taking drugs. I'm not going to push him. If and when he decides to share with me, I'll be here to listen without judgement.

When I return to the living room with coffee and two plates of scrambled eggs Madden is staring blankly at the television, with a glazed expression. *He needs sleep.*

"I wasn't sure how you take your coffee."

"I like my coffee how I like my men," he teases, and I raise one eyebrow as I wait for the punchline. "In my mouth."

My mouth falls open as I grapple for a reaction, but all the blood has rushed away from my brain and straight to my cock. Madden gives me a cheeky grin that tells me he knows exactly what that comment did to me.

With a huff of a laugh and a shake of my head I pass the mug of black coffee to Madden, followed by the scrambled eggs.

"You didn't have to do this. Thank you," he says, gulping down half the mug in an instant.

"Should I hook you up on a coffee I.V.?" I tease.

"Fuck yes," Madden agrees, wiping the back of his hand across his mouth before digging into his eggs with gusto.

I settle onto the empty side of the couch, careful not to crowd him and start in on my own eggs.

Once we're both finished, I take his plate and put them both in the dishwasher. When I return to the living room Madden is draped over half the couch, not leaving much space for me.

"Sorry, don't mean to be a couch hog. I'm kind of half dead." He yawns and moves to sit up.

"You don't have to get up, as long as you don't have any personal space issues." I slide onto the couch and then pull Madden down against my shoulder. He doesn't protest, simply relaxes against my side. I try to ignore the warm fuzzies I'm getting from cuddling a cute guy. I'm closing in on thirty-years-old; shouldn't I be past the butterflies in the stomach stage of my life?

"You can put on anything you want, I'm easy," Madden offers.

I snort a laugh at his double entendre and start searching Netflix for a decent show to binge watch. I get the feeling it's going to be one of those kinds of days.

"You ever watch *The Office*?"

"Hell yeah. Fact: bears eat beets."

"Bears, beets, *Battlestar Galactica*."

We both start cracking up and I click to start the first episode, content to spend the day lazing on the couch with Madden, quoting *The Office.*

Two episodes in and Madden is fast asleep against my chest, I don't even mind the little bit of drool he's leaving behind. I should probably seek therapy. However, it *is* nice to have a crush on a cute guy. Even if nothing can come of it anytime soon.

As he naps, I run a hand up and down his back. Every once in a while, he'll stir and whimper or his body tenses in his sleep. Each time I manage to lull him back to sleep with a few whispered words of comfort. He must be having nightmares. Not surprising after...everything.

Madden

I blink awake against a solid chest, surrounded by the scent of Irish Springs soap, and man.

Last night sleep evaded me, horrific images dancing behind my eyelids every time I closed them. Apparently, all I needed was Thane's strong arms around me to let me get some shut eye.

"Sorry, I fell asleep on you."

"No problem. You're kind of cute when you snore," Thane teases.

"I do not snore."

"You *so* do."

"Shut up." I give his shoulder a playful shove before pushing myself into a seated position and putting a few inches of space between us. I can't imagine how Thane must feel about this arrangement. He went to the club to find a hookup, now I'm living with him. Zero to live in boyfriend in ten seconds flat. Not that I think Thane's my boyfriend...

"Alright, I'm well rested now. What's the plan for the rest of the day?"

"I need to run to the grocery store, want to

come?" Thane suggests.

The thought of going out in public, surrounded by people I don't know, in a crowd...my heart starts to race. I rub my chest, trying to figure out why it's suddenly getting difficult to breathe. Glancing up at Thane I find concern in his deep brown eyes.

"I'm still kind of tired," I manage to choke out.

"Okay. Is there anything specific you want me to get?" he offers.

I shake my head and fight the urge to wrap myself around him and beg him not to go either. What if something happens to him? Instead I wrap my arms around his waist for a brief hug.

Thane gets ready to leave and asks approximately fifty times over a ten-minute time span if I'm okay alone for a little while, and if I *really* don't need anything.

Once he's gone, I hobble down the hallway to my bedroom where I climb under the covers and pull them over my head.

I'm safe here.

I drag in shallow breaths while forcing myself to think happy thoughts. *Chocolate, Blowjobs, sexy baseball butts, puppies, warm showers.* After a few minutes of happy thoughts my heart rate starts to return to normal.

Thane must think I'm a real piece of work, having a panic attack at the mention of a trip to the grocery store. Maybe he didn't notice. Is it possible he believed I was tired?

I peek out from under my covers and find the bottle of Oxy staring at me from the bedside table. It's taunting me, calling out to me with its siren song. *One won't hurt, two won't hurt...*

No!

I tug the covers back over my head and clench my eyes closed as hard as I can, clenching my fists and focusing on the feel of my short nails digging into the palms of my hands.

Ignoring the pain that rocks through me, I roll over so I'm facing away from the nightstand and then I slide out of bed, refusing to turn back and look at the pills. I hobble out of my room, desperate to put space between myself and my temptation.

I ease down on the couch and force myself to count my breaths. When I'm feeling almost normal, I decide I should do something nice for Thane.

Thane

As I walk in the door an hour later a clattering in the kitchen alerts me to a possible problem. I set down the bags of groceries and turn the corner into the kitchen, where I find Madden balancing on one crutch trying to pick up the pans now strewn across the floor.

"What'cha doin'?"

A pink tinge creeps into Madden's cheeks.

"I was trying to cook dinner for us. It's

harder than it seems with only one arm and one leg."

"Imagine that." I offer him a smile before bending down to pick up the pans off the floor. "Let me put the groceries away, then I'll be your sous chef. You can tell me what you need me to do."

Madden's blush deepens but he smiles and nods. I head back to the hallway to pick up the bags I'd left there, and get the items put away before turning back to Madden for my instructions.

"Okay, I was going to make chicken and vegetable stir-fry. So, I need to heat that skillet, and start chopping vegetables, then chicken," Madden explains.

I nod and place the skillet on the stove, then turn to the fridge and pull out a variety of veggies and a package of chicken breasts.

"So, you're hot and you cook. How are you single?" I tease as I begin to chop, with Madden supervising.

"I'm more of a boyfriend guy, I guess. It can be hard to find a guy I'm interested in, who's also looking for more than a hook-up."

My heart stutters at his words and a small smile tugs at my lips. Not that I've traditionally been a *boyfriend* kind of guy, and not that I'm going to make a move on Madden when he's got so much to process right now physically and emotionally. But, it's good to know.

"No offense, but the problem might be that

you were at the club looking for a boyfriend."

Madden chuckles and rolls his eyes at me.

"I wasn't at the club looking for a boyfriend. Just because I prefer boyfriends to hookups doesn't mean I don't get lonely and horny sometimes."

Heat rushes through me at his admission but I force myself not to jump him and cure every bit of loneliness and horniness he's ever felt.

"That makes sense. Been single long?" It's probably too invasive to ask, but fuck it, I'm dying to know.

"A few weeks. I Caught my last boyfriend in bed with another guy."

"That sucks. Dude must've been an idiot."

Madden shrugs and passes me another stack of vegetables to chop.

"It was bullshit he cheated on me. But we were drifting apart. It was one of those relationships where things should've ended long before they did, but you stay together because it's comfortable."

I nod in understanding, ignoring the twinge of jealousy in my gut at the thought of Madden with another man, even if it was before we met.

"What about you? I can't imagine a gorgeous, heroic firefighter like yourself has much trouble keeping his bed warm at night."

I shrug as I move all the chopped vegetables to the side and start slicing the chicken.

"I'm not out at work or anything, or at least

I wasn't," I correct with a laugh. "I'd like to be a boyfriend guy, but it was hard to find a guy willing to put up with being kept a secret."

"I'm sorry you were outed like that."

"Honestly, it's kind of a relief. I spent so long making excuses to myself and telling myself it wasn't the right time. It's better this way. Even if the circumstances suck overall."

"Have you talked to your parents?"

"No," I sigh. "I sent my mom a text letting her know I'm fine and will call her as soon as I can. I think she'll be fine with me being gay. The bigger issue will be that I lied to her for nearly thirty years. She's going to cry, I just know it. I can't stand to make my mother cry."

"Why didn't you tell her sooner?"

"I guess I got used to being in the closet. First it was because I was young and didn't feel ready to be 'out', then I joined the marines and I'm sure you can imagine how that is. After the marines it was the fire department, and that's just as much of a boy's club. I got so used to keeping my private life private. And I've never had a serious boyfriend. I think if I had I probably would've come out to her sooner."

"Makes sense."

"What about you? How'd your parents take it?" As soon as the words are out Madden tenses beside me. I stop chopping and glance up at him. His jaw is tense, his eyes far away.

"Not well," he says after a moment, followed by a humorless laugh. I want to press for more, but it's obvious he's shut down.

"Guess I'll find out soon enough how the guys at work feel about it." I say to take the spotlight off Madden.

"You think they'll be dicks about it?"

"Some probably will. I hope it doesn't get in the way. Trust is important when you're in a dangerous situation."

Madden places a comforting hand on my shoulder but doesn't say any more about it. Instead he instructs me on how he wants the chicken and veggies cooked, and we move on to lighter topics of conversation.

"Do you want to get married?"

"Well, I don't know you that well, but I do like spontaneity so, why not?" Madden teases.

I feel my face flame as I realize how that question sounded.

"I meant in general."

"Oh, in that case…" he laughs, clearly enjoying giving me a hard time. "Yeah, when I meet the right guy, I definitely want to get married."

"Me too."

By the time we sit down to eat we're both laughing and ribbing each other over our differing choices in workout playlists.

"Scoff if you will, but I dare you to put on some Christina Aguilera or Britney Spears and not get lost in the beat," I defend myself. I've never told anyone about my weakness for nineties and early two-thousand pop music and Madden is laughing so hard he's clutching his side and crying.

"I've never heard anything funnier in my life. Oh my god, it hurts to laugh this hard, but I can't stop."

When he finally regains composure, I level him with a sardonic expression.

"And what, do you work out to smart guy?"

"Heavy metal," he responds as though it's the most obvious thing in the world.

"Pop music is better, it's got a better beat to keep you on track," I argue.

"Whatever you say, princess." Madden bursts out laughing again. I can't even be mad when he's enjoying himself this much. I can only imagine the field day he'll have if he catches me belting out some Britney while I shower.

"It's Britney bitch." I whip my head around like I'm flipping long, luxurious hair and Madden laughs so hard he almost falls out of his seat. I lunge forward to steady him so he doesn't cause himself any more damage than he's already suffered.

"You might be my new favorite person," Madden declares once he catches his breath. Warmth spreads through my chest and I smile.

"Back at ya."

CHAPTER 5

Madden

I slept like shit the next three nights in a row. Each day the same as the last, falling asleep on Thane's shoulder the moment he wakes up in the morning. If he minds it he doesn't say anything. But this isn't a sustainable situation. He'll go back to work at some point. What's more, I'll move back to my own place eventually. I need to be able to sleep without the arms of my own personal superhero around me.

When I wake up from my nap on Thursday, I have a missed text from Adam asking if he can stop by. The message is casual but knowing Adam I'm sure he's worried about me. I tell him he can stop by whenever and give him the address.

Twenty minutes later a knock on the front door alerts us to Adam's arrival. Thane gives me a light pat on my good leg and then gets up to let my friend in.

"Hey, dude," Adam greets, sliding onto the couch beside me. I wince as the cushion jostles.

"Want some Tylenol?" Thane offers, noticing my grimace. My mouth falls open in surprise. I guess I shouldn't be shocked that he'd guess that I was avoiding my opiate pain medication specifically. Which means, he's no doubt guessed the reason.

"Yeah, thanks."

Adam eyes me with concern as Thane disappears. If anyone knows about the depths of my drug addiction, it's Adam.

At the age of eighteen, after being kicked out of my parents' house for being gay four years earlier, I found myself chasing any way to mask the pain. I stumbled into Heathens Ink, looking to sell some of my drawings for quick cash. The other tattoo shops in the area would usually buy them for fifty bucks and then hurry me out the door before anyone could be disgusted by the homeless junkie standing in the lobby. I hadn't tried Heathens before because I had seen Adam and thought he was hot. I was intimidated. But I needed a fix bad, and Heathens was right there. So, I walked into the shop and nearly withered instantly under Adam's gaze.

He was in his early twenties at the time but held himself with utter confidence. His deep blue eyes traveled over my skinny, dirty form, sizing me up.

"Can I help you?" He asked, narrowing his eyes at me.

"Um...yeah...uh...I've got, drawings," I stammered, approaching the counter with my sketch book. "To sell, I mean."

Adam crossed his arms over his broad chest and continued to eye me warily. Then I flipped open my sketchbook and his whole demeanor changed.

"Holy shit, you drew this?" He reached for the book and pulled it closer, carefully flipping through the images.

"Yeah."

"You're amazing. You ever think about learning to tattoo?" He raised a bushy eyebrow at me and my mouth went dry.

"Well, yeah. But...I mean....who would offer me an apprenticeship?" I let out a humorless laugh.

"I would," Adam responded with a shrug. "You'd have to get off drugs, of course. Is that a deal breaker?"

"No," I answered, my heart leaping in my chest. This was my chance to turn my life around.

"Alright, here's the deal then, you'll move into my extra bedroom and we'll get you signed up for a drug rehab program. Once you're a month sober you can start your apprenticeship here. If I have any reason to believe you're back on drugs at any time, you're out of the shop and out of my house. Understood?"

"Yes." I nodded with enthusiasm. I couldn't believe this was happening. "I'm gay," I blurted, afraid that if I didn't get that out of the way now it would cause everything to fall apart later.

"That's cool. My best friend, Gage is, too. He works here and lives at my place also, so you'll get to know him well. So, do you have any stuff you'll need to go get or do you want to hang around until I close up shop in an hour and come home with me?"

"Why are you doing this?" I asked warily. No one had ever been that nice to me, not even my own parents.

"You're talented and you sort of remind me of my little brother."

I relaxed a fraction, glad that his answer didn't suggest he was looking for something in exchange for his kindness.

"Don't doubt that I'll throw you right out on your ass if you relapse."

"Understood."

Adam reached out his hand for me to shake.

"Welcome to Heathens Ink."

The rest was history. I'd been tattooing and living with Adam for four years and hadn't touched prescription pain meds- or any other drugs- since that day. There were times I'd been low, and the temptation almost got to be too much. Adam and the family I'd made at Heathens Ink were always there to pull me back from the ledge. If nothing else, the last thing I want is to go through detoxing again. That shit sucked.

"Don't worry, it's plain Tylenol, no codeine," I assure him. Even as I say the words a rush of longing surges through me. *Would it be so bad to have a little?*

"Are you doing okay with...everything?" Adam asks.

"Yeah, haven't touched the shit the hospital sent me home with."

"What about everything else?"

Thane returns with a glass of water and two extra strength Tylenol. My stomach flutters at the caring gesture and I give him a small *thank you* smile before popping the pills and turning back to Adam.

"I'm alright. I'm healing little by little. Thane's taking good care of me."

"Good. When does your physical therapy start?"

"Tomorrow, then I should have a timeline for getting back to work," I assure him.

"Don't worry about that. Your job is there waiting for you, no matter how long it takes. Focus on getting better."

"Thanks, man."

Adam's phone pings with a notification and he quickly whips it out of his pocket and smiles when he sees whoever messaged him.

"Kira?" I ask trying not to sound disapproving. Adam and Kira have had an on again, off again relationship for the past two years and to say that no one at the shop can stand her is an understatement. She's a beautiful girl, but her personality is hot garbage.

"Uh, no," Adam responds after he finishes typing to whoever it was. The look on his face tells me it's probably a girl, and to hear that he might be getting mushy for a girl other than Kira is enough to make me do an internal happy dance. I wait for him to say more, but when he doesn't I decide not to push it.

We settle back and fall into a comfortable silence as a new episode of *Tattoo Nightmares* comes on.

Thane

"Hey, can I talk to you about something?" Madden asks shortly after Adam leaves.

"Of course." I mute the television and turn to give him my attention. He's chewing his bottom lip and his shoulders are tense, but I wait quietly until he's ready to say whatever's on his mind.

"So, I'm assuming you already guessed, but after everything you've done for me, I owe you honesty." He takes a deep breath and holds my gaze as he speaks the next words. "I'm a recovering drug addict. I lived on the streets from age fourteen to eighteen, and during that time I took pretty much any drugs I could get my hands on. My drug of choice was Oxy, whenever I could get it."

His words sink in and I feel my gaze involuntarily dart to his bedroom where I know he has a whole bottle of Oxy from the doctor. Madden tenses when he sees where my gaze has gone, and I immediately feel like an asshole. He admits something major to me and the first thing I do is assume he's popping pills when I'm not looking.

"I haven't taken any. In fact, you should take those from me and flush them."

"Don't you need them for the pain? What if I took them and just gave you one when you really need it?" I suggest.

"I'm afraid to risk it."

I nod in understanding but decide to hang onto the pills just in case. I hate the idea of Madden in pain and not having anything for him. I look at Madden again, trying to picture him as a scared, skinny kid with no one to look out for him. Every cell in my body revolts against the thought. I want to go back in time and find a way to protect him from everything.

"You were homeless when you were a kid?"

"Yeah, I told you my parents didn't take my coming out well," Madden gives me a sad, lopsided smile. "When I was fourteen they caught me kissing my friend Mark. It was my first kiss, actually. They freaked out, they were crazy religious, and told me I could either go to conversion therapy or leave their house and never come back. Even at that age I had an idea what went on in conversion therapy, and I decided to take my chances on the streets."

"That's fucked up. I'm so sorry, Madden." I put my arms around him and do my best to hug away all the horror life has inflicted on him.

"Not going to lie, it fucking sucked. Life hasn't turned out all that bad for me. I've got my job, my friends, and I'm living with a sexy marine." He gives me a flirtatious wink.

"How'd you get off the street?" I ask.

"Adam. I went into Heathens Ink to sell him some of my art for cash so I could buy drugs. He offered me a lifeline. I took it and never looked back."

Now I understand why he was so upset when he got the news he might not be able to use his hand to tattoo anymore. Life has dealt him a shitty hand. From what I know of Madden at this point, if there's any chance of getting full use of his hand back, he'll find a way.

Later that night I decide to bite the bullet and call my mom. After hearing about how Madden's parents took his coming out, I felt like I'd waited long enough to be honest with my own. I know they'll take it fine. If not a little upset that I've been silent so long.

"It's about time," my mom answers after one ring.

"Sorry, I've had a lot going on."

"I know. We saw you on the news. You were at that gay club during the shooting. And your...friend...was shot. Is he okay?"

I take a deep breath, considering my words.

"He's going to be alright. He's staying with me while he's healing. His leg is going to take a while to heal, so I'm helping him out."

"I'm glad he's okay," she says, and then silence stretches out between us. I know what she's waiting for, and what I owe her.

"I'm gay, mom."

"Why didn't you tell me before?" Her voice quivers like she's holding back tears.

"I'm sorry. It was stupid, but I had to keep it quiet at work and everything, so I guess I got used to *not* saying anything about it. I'm sorry."

"I was worried you thought I wouldn't approve," she admits followed by a sniffle.

"No, mom. I knew you would love me no matter what," I promise.

Another sniffle.

"I feel like I've missed out on a huge part of your life. Were there boyfriends I never got to meet? Are there other things I don't know?"

"No one serious. And I swear there's nothing else."

Then a sob comes through the phone and I drop down on the bed, rubbing my free hand over my face as she begins to weep.

"All the times I asked if you had a girlfriend, you could have told me. I don't even know my son. I'm the worst mother. I should've seen the signs. I should've known."

"Mom, listen to me," I say in a soothing tone. "You are a great mom. Me not telling you had nothing to do with you, and everything to do with me. The time never felt right. And I realize now what a bad excuse that is, because I have had not one but two careers where I risk my life on a daily basis. I hate the idea that I could've died and you never would've known." It's my turn to choke back a sob. I can't believe how selfish I was, hiding such an important part of myself from my parents all this time. Any why? I knew they wouldn't be like Madden's—or so many others—parents. I *knew* they'd accept me.

"Promise you'll be honest with me from now on?"

"I promise," I agree without hesitation. Having her know is like a weight off my shoulders I hadn't realized was there. "Do you want to grab dad so I can tell him too?"

"You're on speaker, he heard you."

"Oh. Sorry, dad. I should've said something sooner."

"I understand, son. As long as you know we always support you," my dad says.

"I know, dad."

"So, is it serious with this man? Can your father and I meet him?"

"We're not dating. I met him at the club that night for the first time."

"You like him?" she presses. Just like my mom. Now that she knows I like men instead of women she jumps right back into pressing for me to find someone special to settle down with.

"I do, he's a great guy. But he's healing and it's not the right time. Maybe eventually…"

"You're quite a catch, he'd be crazy not to be interested," my mom declares.

"Thanks mom."

We make small talk for another twenty minutes and then I let them go with a promise to call more often and to keep them updated on how Madden is healing.

I strip my shirt and jeans off and climb into my bed. I have no idea what I was thinking when I bought a king size bed. It's too big for one person. I allow my mind to conjure the fantasy of having Madden in my bed. My heart aches at how perfect it would feel to have him here, spooned against me as we lay and talk about everything and nothing until we both fall asleep.

I hate the thought of Madden sitting up all night, tormented by nightmares. He hasn't asked for anything, though, and I don't want to overstep or push him. Maybe I can come up with a way to convince him that we should share a bed. Strictly platonically, of course. He seems to sleep better when I'm there. I want to chase all his nightmares away for him. I want to rescue him from anything that could ever hurt him.

Without my permission my mind starts to wander from platonic to...not so platonic. My skin prickles hot as my mind conjures thoughts of Madden's skin. Of how it would feel under my fingertips and taste against my tongue. I'm a horrible person for entertaining these desires, but it's out of my control as my cock stiffens and my hand moves unconsciously to grasp it.

I gasp and buck my hips as I swipe my thumb through the pre-cum oozing from the tip and spread it around. The images in my mind keep playing, flashes of Madden's own hard cock against my lips, my tongue, pressing into the back of my throat.

I bite down on my fist to stifle my cry as my other hand pumps in rough jerks. My balls ache as they draw tight to my body. God it doesn't feel like it's enough. Madden's words from the night we met fill my mind. *If you're looking for a guy to bend over, I'm not him. I'd be happy to flip you for it.*

This time I bite my tongue against the moan that threatens to escape. Fuck, I want that. In general I will bottom, but I'm not crazy about it. But, goddamn do I want Madden to fuck me. I want to feel him filling me and dominating me until I can't even remember a time when he wasn't inside me.

I shove my middle finger into my mouth to wet it as I continue to fuck my fist. Then, I spread my legs and bend my knees. I haven't fingered myself in forever so when my damp finger meets my hole I clench without meaning to. I forgot how sensitive that area is. I force myself to slow down a little, jerking my cock slower as I circle and tease my asshole until I'm shaking and gasping for breath.

"Oh god, oh fuck, fuck, yeah," I whimper. My whole body tenses and lights with pleasure. My toes curl and I arch up off the bed as I come harder than I ever have before. Ropes of hot seed shoot over my abs, chest, and even reach my neck.

Out of breath and sticky the only coherent

thought in my head is that if I can have that mind blowing of an orgasm thinking of Madden, what would it be like to let him fuck me?

Madden

"Can I ask you something?" I ask over breakfast the next morning. After another sleepless night the only thing I can think to help give my mind some peace, is to get some answers.

"Of course."

"I haven't watched the news or looked it up. I've been too afraid of reliving it. What happened? Did they get the guy? Why'd he do it? How many people died?" I shoot off my questions rapid fire.

A frown tugs at Thane's lips. He sets down his mug of coffee and faces me to answer my questions.

"Ten people died, fifteen more were injured. The guy who did it shot himself before the police could get to him, so we don't know his motives for certain. Most of the news sites are saying that his parents were very religious, his friends saying he never dated. They're speculating that he was a self-hating, closeted gay man."

My gut wrenches. How easily that fate could've been mine. If I'd let my parents manipulate me and shame me into hiding in the closet how would I have turned out? Was this man forced to endure conversion therapy? Was he subjected to electroshock or abusive "therapy" until his mind couldn't take any more and he snapped? Pity and hatred mingle in my gut making me both sick and sad.

"Are you okay?" Thane's eyebrows draw together as he looks me over.

"Kind of," I lie. "Not really," I amend after a moment.

"Don't take offense to this at all, but maybe you should think about talking with a therapist? It can help to talk out your feelings with someone after a traumatic event."

"I'm fine," I snap. If I can survive being disowned by my parents, living on the streets for four years, kicking a drug habit, and live through a shooting I can get over a few nightmares.

I can feel Thane's eyes on me, but he doesn't say any more or push the issue, for which I'm grateful.

My hand twitches for a pencil. When my emotions are this chaotic, I usually use my art to work through it. I can't. That fucker took my art from me, possibly forever.

Then, a familiar rolling itch creeps along under my skin. *Did Thane flush my Oxy or is it sitting up in his bedroom right now?*

I would fucking kill for some happy right about now.

CHAPTER 6

Madden

"Are you sure you don't want me to stay?" Thane asks me for the umpteenth time as he pulls his car up in front of the physical therapist's office.

"I'll be fine. Go grab a cup of coffee or something and meet me back here in an hour," I assure him with more confidence than I'm feeling. What if the PT tells me I won't be able to tattoo or draw ever again? I could give a shit about my leg. It would suck to not have full use of my leg, but I'd adapt. Without my art I have nothing worth living for. Alright, I'm being dramatic, but my point stands.

My stomach knots as I maneuver myself out of the car and hobble up to the building. This is the first time I've been in public since I went home with Thane, and every cell in my body feels wrong. My heart thunders and my lungs feel like they've constricted, making it nearly impossible to draw in a full breath.

"Can I help you sir?" A friendly looking woman asks me. I blink in confusion. I didn't realize I'd made it to the check in desk.

"Uh, yeah, I'm Madden Brody. I have an appointment with Mark Gregory."

"Okay, why don't you have a seat and fill out this paperwork and he'll be with you shortly."

"Uh, paperwork might not be too easy," I say, giving the receptionist a wry smile. She glances at my chart and must realize that part of the reason I'm here is because my right hand is practically useless at the moment.

"Of course, I'm so sorry. I'll help you fill these out."

"Thanks. Can I ask what the co-pay is? I probably should've asked sooner..."

"There won't be any charge. Mark is donating his services to the victims of the nightclub shooting," she assures me with a warm smile.

"For real?" I gape at her in disbelief.

"Yes, this hit home for him and he wanted to give something back." She hands me a clipboard with some standard medical forms, and I shuffle to the nearest chair and collapse down into it, leaning my crutch up against the wall.

By the time we get the forms filled out a man in his early thirties peeks his head out from the back and calls my name.

"It's nice to meet you, Madden," he greets me with a warm smile. He looks entirely too young to be a physical therapist, but he also looks like a bit of a hard-ass. Former military would be my guess.

"Likewise. I want to thank you for doing this without charge, it means a lot."

"Don't mention it, and please call me Mark," he waves it off. "My younger brother was the victim of a hate crime. He died five years ago," the doctor leads me into his office, and I notice a picture on his desk of a younger version of himself, next to a skinny kid. I'm guessing that was his brother.

"I'm so sorry to hear that."

"We're not here to talk about my tragic backstory, Madden. We're here to get you back in full physical form. I like to start by having my patients tell me their goals for therapy."

"I need to get full use of my right hand back. I'm an artist; I need my fine motor skills."

"Okay." He nods and fixes me with a stern look. "This isn't going to be easy. I hope you're ready for a lot of hard work."

"Yes sir,"

"That's what I like to hear, now let's get started."

The next hour is spent with Mark showing me exercises for my leg as well as for my arm to strengthen my hand. It's hard to believe it's possible to lose so much muscle tone so quickly. I've only been taking it easy for ten days, but I'm exhausted and sore as hell by the end of the hour.

It feels good to be sweating and working hard again. Maybe I'll manage to sleep tonight after getting some exercise in.

Thane

Leaving Madden alone feels all kinds of wrong. The last thing I want to do is force my help on him. If he says he's fine, then I need to let him be. That's easier said than done. Protecting people is like a compulsion for me. And, that instinct- for whatever reason- seems to be in overdrive when it comes to Madden. I did a piss-poor job of protecting him that night, and I'm never going to let that happen again.

Not that I'm particularly religious but I send up some happy thoughts into the universe that the PT will have something positive to say about his hand. After everything he told me about how much his art and tattooing means to him. I can't imagine he'd have a good reaction if he was told he'll never make art in the same way again.

I pull into a coffee shop a few blocks from Madden's appointment and go inside to kill some time.

When I approach the barista to place my order, she's all fluttering eyelashes and coy smiles. The attention I tend to garner from women is even worse if I wear one of my fire department t-shirts. I feel a little bad for the poor girls. In my defense, it's not like I encourage them.

I offer her a friendly smile and order a black coffee with room for cream and sugar. Then I sit down and play on my phone for a while until five minutes before Madden's appointment is supposed to be over.

I open my Facebook app for the first time

in weeks and find that I have hundreds of notifications. It seems like everyone I know had something to say about the incident, from calling me a hero to calling me a fag, my wall is full of posts from acquaintances and strangers alike.

After reading a few I click the notification tab to mark all as read and decide not to look at the rest. Even the positive messages are emotionally exhausting.

I look up Madden's Facebook to see if he's getting the same thing I am. He is, but his posts seem to be overwhelmingly positive and supportive. So many people wishing him well, telling him they hope he heals quickly, asking who the 'hunky man' was carrying him out of the club.

Madden hasn't responded to any of the posts. He must be avoiding social media at the moment, too.

I close the app and put my phone back in my pocket. When I look up, I notice two teenage boys at the table next to me whispering and sneaking glances at me.

"Ask him," one of the guys whispers loud enough for me to hear and gives his friend a shove. The other boy laughs at his friend and flips his bangs out of his eyes before leaning in my direction.

"Excuse me."

I raise my eyebrows and make eye-contact.

"Are you the guy who saved that other guy at the nightclub shooting?" he asks.

My face flames. I'm used to saving lives. I'm not used to be recognized in public for it.

"Um...yeah, that's me," I confirm with a small smile.

"Oh my god, that was the *most* romantic thing of all time. Seriously, like, ever," the other man gushes, looking at me with hearts in his eyes.

I clear my throat and nod. God this is awkward. I don't know how to be gay in public. How do people figure this stuff out?

"Is your boyfriend okay?" the first guy asks. My heart stutters at hearing Madden called my boyfriend, but I don't correct him. I kind of like the sound of it.

"He will be."

"Oh my gosh, true love goals, for real."

"Thanks," I nod again and sip my coffee, trying to figure out what the correct response is. "Well, I'd better go. I have to pick my *boyfriend* up from physical therapy."

Both men "aww" and then wave at me as I walk away.

When I pull up to the building Madden is leaning against the stone half-wall out front, with his crutches leaned beside him. I park the car along the curb and get out to help him in.

"How'd it go?"

"Good. The PT seems cool. It's going to be a

lot of hard work."

"Oh yeah. I had to have physical therapy a few years ago after the floor caved in while I was evacuating a house. Anyway, I landed on my back and fucked it up pretty good. Had to have six weeks of PT and I felt like I was back in basic all over again."

Madden laughs as he settles into his seat and I point the car toward home.

"So, what did he think about your hand? Does he think you'll get full use back?" I know his art was Madden's biggest concern. And, after everything he told me the other day about his past, I get why it's so important to him.

"Yeah, he said with hard work I should be able to get there. He did warn me that with the nerve damage I might always have unsteady hands which I may have to learn to compensate for with my art."

"If anyone can do it, you can," I assure him. "Hey, we should go out and do something. What about dinner or a movie?" I'm aware how date-like that sounds, but it doesn't stop me from wanting to take Madden somewhere fun.

Out of the corner of my eye I notice him tense.

"I'm kind of tired."

Something about his tone of voice makes me think he's being less than honest. I knew that sound too date-like. Now he must think I'm trying to take advantage of him.

"What if we order Chinese food and binge watch *Sons of Anarchy*?" He suggests and the tightness in my chest loosens a fraction.

"Sounds good," I agree. Madden relaxes again in his seat, letting out a quiet sigh.

Madden

As soon as Thane suggested going out somewhere my whole body went ice cold. My airway had started to squeeze shut and I knew I was seconds away from a full-on panic attack. What if we go somewhere and something happens again? There are shootings every day, in so many types of locations. Nowhere is safe. Movie theaters, shopping malls, restaurants, fuck even parks. *Nowhere is safe. That's not true- I'm safe at home with Thane.*

Once we're back home Thane pulls out his phone and orders food while I get comfortable on the couch and pull up the second season of *Sons of Anarchy*. We discovered the other day that we both share a deep affection for Charlie Hunnam and decided to re-watch SOA together from the beginning

When Thane slides onto the couch beside me I let out a breath I hadn't realized I'd been holding. For the first time since we left the house this morning for my appointment, I feel comfortable and secure. The question of how and when I'll ever feel safe going outside again tugs at the back of my mind, but I shove it away.

"It's weird, I don't even know where you

grew up," I say after Thane is settled in.

"I grew up in Oregon, near Portland. My parents still live there."

"So, what brought you to Seattle?"

"After I got out of the marines, I decided I wanted to be a firefighter so I looked for a community college with the courses I would need. I wanted to be close enough to my parents to have the chance to visit whenever, but didn't want to be so close that they would be up my ass, you know?"

I nod in understanding.

"What about you?" he asks.

"Texas."

"Really? You don't have an accent."

"Yeah, I worked hard to lose that fucking twang. I didn't want any reminder of that ass backward state. Sometimes, if I talk to someone who has an accent, I'll slip into it without thinking."

"That sounds kind of...hot." I can feel Thane's gaze on me, heating my blood. *Is that a come on? Should I make a move?*

I risk a glance at him, but he's already looking back at the television. Making me think the comment was innocuous, I'm sure I was reading more into it than he intended.

"So, why'd you join the marines?"

"Honestly? I was eighteen, had no idea what I wanted to do with my life, and being a marine seemed kind of badass," Thane answers with a shrug.

"You joined the marines and risked your life because it sounded badass?"

"Yup, which is why eighteen-year-olds shouldn't be allowed to make any decisions."

"That's fair," I agree with a laugh. "So, why a fireman, then?"

"Well, as ill-conceived as the Marines idea was, it turned out that saving people felt like my calling. So, I kicked around a few ideas and by the time my time in the Marines was up I settled on firefighter."

"You're amazing. I feel like a slacker next to you, making doodles with my life," I lament.

"You make the world more beautiful. That is a wonderful calling."

My throat tightens at Thane's praise.

"You have any siblings?" I ask him, desperate to know everything there is to know about him.

"No, just me. You?"

"No, thank god."

Although, maybe my parents would've been perfectly lovely to a straight child. Even before they caught me kissing another boy, they could tell I was different. That was why they forced me to memorize bible verses. That was why they sent me to a 'therapist' who spent one day a week for years telling me that sex was filthy and wrong, and even more so when it occurred between two men. Catching me kissing Mark was the last straw.

"Favorite food?" I ask to change the subject.

"Cupcakes," Thane answers with a dreamy smile, to which I snort a laugh. Big, manly marine loves cupcakes. "Biggest fear?"

I hesitate to answer. If you'd asked me six weeks ago what my biggest fear was relapse. Even now, that's a terrifying and very real horror. I'd face another round of detoxing and rehab, rather than taking a second turn at the wrong end of a gunman. I swallow around the lump in my throat, unable to form the words I fall back on humor instead.

"Nicolas Cage, the actor," I answer with faux seriousness. Thane laughs and shakes his head at me. "What about you? What are you afraid of?"

"Losing someone I'm responsible for," he responds without hesitation. "It's happened before, and it'll happen again. It keeps me awake at night all the same."

I put a comforting hand on his and shift closer to rest my head on his shoulder. He lifts an arm and puts it around my shoulders. I sigh as I settle against his strong body.

I'm safe here.

That thought is like a warm blanket, wrapping around me and making my eyelids heavy and my brain foggy. I relax against Thane's strong body. *He'll protect me.*

Thane

Within minutes Madden is fast asleep against my chest, snuffling and snoring in the most adorable way. I brush a brief kiss against his forehead, and he nuzzles closer still fast asleep. I'd give anything to take his pain away.

What would it be like if things had ended differently that night? I allow my mind to wander into a daydream where there was no shooter. Madden and I came back to my house that night and made love until the sun came up and then slept soundly in my bed until the afternoon. We'd have woken up and lazed away the afternoon talking in bed, getting to know everything about each other. Then I'd have asked for his phone number and promised to call. I wouldn't have been able to wait even a whole day to text him and let him know he was on my mind.

I glance down now at his sleeping form in my arms and my heart hurts. Can we still get to that place eventually? I'm not in any rush. I'm happy to wait as long as it takes for Madden to be physically and mentally well. And then...maybe someday...who knows.

Ever since I came out to my mom the other day, she's been texting me asking how Madden is doing several times a day. It's kind of cute how much she cares, even though she hasn't met him yet. Would Madden want to meet my parents one day?

It's silly to even think about, we're not even dating, after all. I've never had a serious boyfriend. I've never met a guy I wanted to introduce my parents to. There've been guys I've dated. It's just that none of them ever sparked that fire in me that said this could be something special. With Madden...Well, I don't know him as well as I want to yet, but *this could be something special.*

Madden murmurs in his sleep and shifts around against me. I rub my hand up and down his back and whisper soothing words into his ear to calm him. He settles again and I know in this moment that I'm a goner. I'm helpless against falling for this man.

CHAPTER 7

Madden

"Will you be okay? I won't be back until tomorrow afternoon," Thane reminds me as he fidgets with his shoelace, appearing to be stalling for time.

The past three weeks have flown by in a blur of physical therapy and lack of sleep. I'm getting physically stronger, though not as quickly as I'd like. My PT keeps reminding me that it's not going to get better overnight and that I need to be patient and continue to work hard. That's easy for him to say, I can still barely use my right fucking hand.

"Yes, I'll be fine. Royal is going to be here in less than an hour and he's going to stay the night to keep me company. Don't worry about me, keep yourself safe and I'll see you tomorrow." The urge to lean forward and brush a sweet kiss to his lips like a boyfriend or a husband would, nearly overwhelms me. I bite down hard on my lip and duck my face to resist the urge to press my mouth to his.

"Alright," Thane clears his throat and finally stands to full height. "Text me if there's an emergency or anything. I'll see you tomorrow."

I watch him retreat out the door before hobbling toward the living room using my crutch.

Less than an hour after Thane left for work there's a knock at the front door.

"Come in," I yell from the couch.

Moments later Royal strides in with a big smile on his face. Royal is gorgeous, and I can see why Thane was worried about my relationship with him at first. He's got a buzz cut on the sides of his head with it long on top, and a full, sexy beard. The thing about Royal that garners the most attention from male and female admirers is his full sleeve tattoos. That, and he's a huge flirt.

"Hey stud, how're you feeling?" He asks as he eases onto the couch beside me.

"Eh, getting there," I answer with a shrug. I'm not about to dump all over him about the lack of sleep I've been getting or the persistent ache in my leg.

"So, what's up with you and the sexy fireman?" Royal asks, waggling his eyebrows suggestively.

I roll my eyes at my friend, mostly annoyed by the reminder that *nothing* is going on between Thane and me.

"Nothing. He's become a good friend, that's it."

"Bullshit," Royal declares. "I saw how he was looking at you in the hospital. He has the major hots for you."

I shrug, refusing to let him plant the seed of hope in my mind that'll only lead to disappointment and rejection.

"I thought so too, but now I think I looked a lot better as a club hook-up than I do as a live-in boyfriend. He hasn't made a single move since I moved in. I mean, he flirts, but that's it."

"Did you ever think that he's not a complete asshole who's going to jump a guy who was recently shot repeatedly? He's probably giving you time to heal, waiting for you to make the first move," Royal argues with an air of condescension, like it's the most obvious thing in the world.

"Maybe. There's a lot going on for both of us so it's not really the right time anyway. Like you said, I'm trying to heal both physically and mentally. And, he wasn't even out until the *incident*. I'm sure he's got a lot to process. I'm not going to push anything. If it happens, it happens. If not, I'm glad to have a friend like Thane."

"You're crazy. If I was rooming with a hot piece of ass like that, I'd be all over it."

"So, go find a hot piece of ass. You're gorgeous, Royal. And you're just the right amount of an asshole that gets both guys and girls all aflutter," I tease.

"Fuck off," he responds with a laugh.

"I wish I could, but my right hand is still kinda out of commission."

"Dude, you can't jack off?" The look of horror on Royal's face is priceless, like I just told him anal sex was punishable by death.

"I can go leftie, but it doesn't get the job done the same."

"That's the saddest thing I've ever heard, but it's also the perfect line to use on Thane. *Excuse me, but I seem to need a hand.*"

"In your mind life is basically a giant porno, isn't it?"

"More or less," Royal answers with a smirk.

Thane

I hop out of my SUV at the firehouse, my muscles twitching in anticipation. I'm glad I had the down time to help Madden settle in, but I'm more than ready to be back in action.

I shove my keys into my pocket and hustle up the steps to the common room to report for my shift.

When I step in, I find five guys sitting around watching TV, waiting for their shift to end. Hayden is the first one to look in my direction, and his eyes light up when he does.

"Grayson, dude." Hayden jumps up and pulls me into a hug, giving me a few firm slaps on the back, total bro hug style. "How are you feeling, man?"

"I'm alright," I assure him.

"And Madden?" he asks. I blink back my shock at hearing my coworker ask about a man I'm...seeing? Not really, but as far as Hayden knows I am.

"He's healing. Long road ahead of him to get back to full speed, but he's getting stronger every day. Thanks for asking."

Hayden gives my shoulder a quick, reassuring squeeze before going to sit back down on the couch. As he does, I notice that the looks I'm getting from the other four guys range from cautiously awkward to downright hostile.

The air hangs heavy as everyone waits for someone else to say something first.

"Good to have you back, Grayson," Xander, a rookie, finally breaks the silence.

"Thanks, it's good to be back."

"Grayson, my office please," the chief calls out, to my relief, allowing me the opportunity to walk away from this awkward situation.

I hurry down the hall to his office and greet the middle-aged man I've come to know and respect. He reaches his hand out to shake mine.

"Glad to have you back."

"Glad to be back, sir."

He gestures towards the chair opposite his desk and I plop down in it.

"How are you? Head clear and ready to return to work? Because I can't have you out there in a crisis if you aren't one hundred and ten percent." His tone is firm, but I can see the concern in his eyes. Not for my job performance, but for my personal well-being.

"I'm one hundred and fifty percent, sir," I assure him without hesitation.

"Good." He nods and then his gaze becomes somewhat guarded as he appears to be searching for his next words. "I want you to know that this station has a policy of inclusion. Your, ah, preferences have no bearing on how you'll be treated as a firefighter."

"I appreciate that, sir." There's a swelling of gratitude in my chest. It's clear the chief isn't fully comfortable with the situation, but he's making a point to let me know this won't affect my job. That's more than I ever hoped for, especially when I was in the marines.

"That being said, not all of the guys seem to be immediately receptive to the, um, information. If anyone gives you any trouble, you let me know."

"Thank you," I say again, swallowing past the lump in my throat.

Madden

I blink awake against a chest that's all wrong. I take a deep breath and smell cigarette smoke rather than the warm, spicy scent I've come to associate with Thane.

"Finally waking up sleeping beauty?" Royal asks with humor in his voice. "I love you and everything, man. But you snore like a motherfucker."

"Fuck you, I do not." I shove myself away from him and rub the sleep from my eyes. The last thing I remember was watching *Entourage* so I'm assuming I must've passed the fuck out on him at some point.

"You so do," he argues with a chuckle. Then he turns a more serious gaze on me. "You sleeping well?"

I snort a laugh and give him a wry smile.

"Let's put it this way, *His name was Tyler Durden*."

"Am I supposed to know what that means?"

"Are you shitting me? *Fight Club*?"

"Haven't seen it," Royal admits with a shrug. My mouth falls open and I grab the controller from his hand.

"We're watching it right now. I can't believe you've never seen *Fight Club*. I'm almost certain that's an offense they can have your balls revoked for."

"Alright, we'll watch it," Royal agrees with a laugh. "But, since I didn't get the reference I don't have the answer to my question. Are you not sleeping?"

"Not so much. Every time I close my eyes I'm there again. And sometimes..."

"What?"

"Sometimes I'm the shooter. It's fucked up."

"Why would you be the killer?" Royal cocks his head to one side.

"I don't know. I guess on some level I feel like it could've been me. Like, I don't know, if I'd let my parents send me to conversation therapy and it made my brain snap or something. It's stupid."

Royal's concern appears to deepen as a little furrow appears between his eyebrows.

"Maybe you should see someone. You know, someone to talk to," Royal suggests.

I bristle at the suggestion.

"I don't need to see a fucking shrink. I'm fine. I'll sleep when I sleep."

The shock is easy to read on Royal's face. I don't think he's ever seen me as anything but chill. I'm not about to dump all my shit on him about why I won't see a therapist.

Thane

I never minded doing the 24 on, 48 off thing before. In fact, it was always kind of nice to have a weekend after every day of work. Being away from Madden for a full day was more difficult than I'd anticipated. He's a grown man. I understand that he can take care of himself. But I *want* to be there to take care of him. I couldn't stop wondering if Royal was making sure Madden was sleeping and eating in my absence.

"Worried about your man?" Hayden asks, sitting down on the bench press next to the one I'm using.

I grunt in response. Don't get me wrong, I'm glad Hayden's being so cool about everything. Talking about a guy with a coworker, however, is going to take some getting used to.

"You know you can talk to me, right? My brother is gay."

I grunt again before sliding the weight into the cradle. Sitting up I wipe the sweat from my face and glance over at Hayden.

"Thanks, man. It's weird to talk about, that's all. I appreciate you being cool."

"Jesus, is this gay shit all we're going to talk about from now on?" Brad gripes as he saunters into the station gym and hops on the nearest treadmill. I do my best to hide my grimace. It doesn't surprise me that Brad's going to be a homophobic dick. He's always been an asshole, constantly making sexist and racist comments. Doesn't surprise me that he's going for the hateful hat trick.

"Nobody asked you," Hayden snaps back at Brad before I can say anything. I give Hayden an appreciative nod before heading out of the weight room and back to the living room. I grab my phone off the coffee table and see a text from Madden.

Madden: Don't want to bug you, just wanted to assure you I'm still alive and well. I know you worry ;)

I chuckle, feeling warmth spread through my chest.

Thane: Don't lie, you miss me

Madden: maybe a little

Madden: Luckily Royal is pretty good company. Or he will be once he shuts up about jerking off.

Thane: LOL, do I even want to know?

Madden: Haha. No, probably not

I can't decide if I'm jealous or turned on by Madden's comment. He said there was nothing between him and Royal, and I have no reason to doubt that. Not that I have any claim to Madden. Not yet, anyway. One day, hopefully.

Thane: Ok, you have me curious. Why won't he shut up about jerking off?

Madden: ...um, well, I kind of mentioned that with my right hand out of commission I can't.

I bite back a groan that threatens to erupt. Fuck, the thought of Madden stretched out, naked in his bed, cock hard, dripping, and in need of relief.

Thane: Well, I did promise to help you with anything you need. You know where to find me ;)

Madden: Tease

My fingers itch to type back just how serious the offer is. The last thing I want to do is make things weird. There'll be time for this when he's better.

CHAPTER 8

Thane

I try not to feel too disappointed that Madden is asleep when I get home. Royal is sitting on the couch watching the end of *Fight Club*.

"Good movie," I say.

"Yeah, I never saw it before. Brad Pitt is hot as hell in this movie, in a weird sociopath kind of way."

I nod in agreement.

"Is Madden sleeping?"

"Yeah, when he fell asleep on me a second time I woke him up and took his ass to bed. Is he doing okay?" Royal asks, gnawing at his bottom lip as his eyebrows draw together.

"He's coping."

"I'm worried that he's not sleeping. He's not...um...did he take his pain meds?" Royal rubs the back of his neck and glances towards Madden's bedroom like he's afraid of being caught talking about him.

"He hasn't relapsed. I'd like him to be sleeping better, but he's been through a trauma, I'm sure he'll be back to himself in no time."

Royal looks skeptical but doesn't argue.

"Alright, I guess I'll get out of your hair. Call me if you or Madden need anything, okay?"

"Thanks."

Once I show Royal out, I head upstairs to my own bed.

The sound of panicked cries pull me from my sleep. I bolt up in my bed and look around the dark room, trying to orient myself. Another guttural scream pierces the otherwise quiet house. *Madden*.

When I'd gotten home from my shift, I'd looked in on him and found him fast asleep. I was happy he was finally getting some rest.

I fling my comforter aside and stumble out of bed, pausing only to pull on a pair of red boxer briefs from the floor. And in record time I'm standing outside Madden's bedroom door.

His wails have faded to whimpers as I ease his bedroom door slowly open. As I suspected he's asleep, but clearly not soundly. He thrashes and mewls, trapped— no doubt— in a horrible nightmare.

I edge quietly onto the bed beside him and put my hand gingerly on his bare back. Madden startles awake with a gasp.

"Shh, it's just me. You're okay. You were having a bad dream," I assure him, with gentle pressure on his skin to help ground him in the here and now.

"Thane?" he croaks in a weary voice.

"Yeah, I'm here," I coo.

Without warning Madden's arms are around my waist, dragging me down beside him. When he buries his face against my naked chest I can feel his whole body still trembling from the trauma of his dream. I'm more than happy to wrap my arms around him and hold him safe and secure against me.

"Sorry, you must think I'm a big baby."

"Not at all. Do you want to talk about it?" I offer, one hand still stroking his back and the other solidly around his hips.

"It was that night. Every time I close my eyes I'm back there. But this time you can't get close enough to save me. A faceless man stands over me and just keeps shooting. I could feel every bullet as it pierced my skin."

My gut clenches. What I wouldn't give to take those memories and fears from him and bear them myself.

"You're safe, I promise. I will *always* save you," I vow, my arms tightening around him.

Madden's breath catches in his chest and he pulls back to gaze up at me with hope and desire.

"Take the pain away, Thane?" he pleads, his fingers tugging gently on my chest hair as he curls his fingers and presses closer.

"How, sweetheart? Tell me how and I'll give you anything." I want him to mean what I think he means. But I can't afford to misunderstand. The last thing Madden needs is for me to make an unwelcome advance on him when he's physically and emotionally vulnerable.

Madden's answer comes in the form of his hot lips against mine. I still in surprise as a taste that is pure Madden assaults my senses. It only takes a fraction of a second for my brain and body to catch up to the moment. I part my lips and deepen the kiss, allowing myself to feel all the things I'd shoved aside after the shooting. All of the anticipation and burning lust I felt the first time we kissed crash over me like a wave.

Madden rolls his hips, his throbbing erection to line up with mine. I groan against his lips and use one hand to grasp his perky ass and the other one to hitch his leg around my waist. Madden gasps, but this time it's not the good kind of gasp.

"Oh shit, I'm sorry I got caught up and forgot about your ankle. It probably hurts to hitch around my leg like that."

"I'm okay, just go gentle," Madden assures me, grabbing the back of my head and dragging me back in for another kiss.

No, kiss doesn't even do it justice. He *possesses* me. Madden's tongue tangles with mine, his lips firm and commanding, hands holding me in place. The dominance of Madden's embrace has my cock pulsing with the need for release.

More carefully this time I maneuver him

onto his back and settle over him. He moans in approval and thrusts his shaft against mine again making me nearly lose my mind. The fabric of both of our boxers are thin. So, despite us not being naked yet, I can feel the ridge of his head sliding against mine in a way that's sending jolts of pleasure straight through my cock.

"God, Thane," Madden moans, fingers clawing at my ass as he tries to shove my underwear off. "I need you. Please."

I need you. Are there any sweeter words in the English language? And when they're uttered as a breathless plea, impossible to deny.

"I don't want to hurt you," I pull back and kiss down his neck tenderly. His chest rises and falls with ragged breaths, his body writhing beneath me. "Let me suck you, and then when you're healed, if you still want to, we can do anything else you want."

"No, I need you," Madden argues, eyes dark with longing.

I graze his peaked nipple with my teeth and he lets out another desperate cry. Another compromise occurs to me that makes my cock jump in anticipation.

"Okay, then let me ride you. That'll be easier on your leg than getting on all fours or trying to get in position to take me."

"Fuck, yeah, let's do that," he agrees, reaching between us to palm my cock, as I manage to get my boxer briefs all the way off and then focus on his.

"Oh, damn, I'm going to have to run back upstairs for supplies. Hang tight, okay?"

Madden nods and I reluctantly jump off the bed and sprint upstairs, erection swaying comically in the open air as I hurry to get lube and condoms and get back downstairs before Madden changes his mind.

When I make it back, I find Madden sprawled out on his bed, his cock jutting proudly upward as he works it with his left hand. A bead of pre-cum glistens at the tip and he catches it with his thumb on the next upstroke. My mouth waters at the sight, straight out of my own mental porn.

Tossing the items on the bed beside him I settle between his legs and bury my face in the juncture of his thighs, inhaling his intoxicating scent. I snake my tongue out and tease the sensitive skin between his balls and his ass.

Madden whimpers and clutches at my short hair. I reach for his dick and bat his own hand away so I can take over the job of stroking him while I continue to lavish his sack with my tongue.

"Thane, stop. Please. I want to cum inside you," he protests feebly as I suck one of his balls between my lips.

My ass clenches expectantly and I drag myself away from the task at hand...or rather, at mouth.

I move up his body so I can straddle his hips and I hand him the bottle of lube.

"I don't usually do this, so take it easy. Okay?"

Madden pauses as he takes the proffered bottle from my hand, and he gazes up at me with concern.

"We don't *have* to do this. I mean, if it's not what you're into I'm perfectly happy to do something else. I want you to feel good."

"I said I don't usually do this, not that I don't want to. I've wanted this with you since the minute I laid eyes on you."

"Really?"

I can't help but laugh at Madden's surprise.

"Why is that hard to believe? I think I was pretty clear that night about my intentions."

"You were, but then after everything else you never made a move again or anything. I guess I figured you weren't that interested after all," Madden admits.

"Baby, did you ever stop to think that I didn't want to add to everything else you were coping with? What you needed was a friend, not some guy trying to get in your pants."

"And now?" He asks with a smirk as he opens the bottle of lube and pours a generous amount on his fingers and begins to rub them together to warm it up.

"Now you're trying to get into *my* pants, and I'm more than happy to let you," I tease with a nip to his ear.

As I lick and suck along his jaw, Madden's fingers slid along the cleft of my ass until they reach my hole. I tense at the unfamiliar sensation. Rather than go right for it and shove his fingers in like some other guys who've made a go of it, Madden carefully circles my entrance, teasing and enticing me until I relax enough that he can start to inch one finger in.

I clench at the slight burn, but Madden continues his patient pace.

"Uh, normally I'm pretty good at multitasking, but my hand..." Madden trails off, his tone apologetic. The laugh that escapes me turns to a moan as he works his finger deeper. Taking his hint, I wrap a hand around my cock and stroke myself slowly.

"Oh fuck, that feels good," I murmur, relaxing enough to begin to enjoy it. By the time a second finger joins the first I'm alternating between thrusting into my hand and impaling myself on his fingers and begging him for more.

"You're so sexy. So perfect. Want you so bad," Madden murmurs against my neck.

When he starts to ease his finger out, I cry out in protest.

"I need a freehand, babe, to put a condom on," he reasons with a smirk.

"No," I argue, reaching for a condom and tearing the package open with my teeth before quickly sheathing him. Next, I grab the bottle of lube and apply a generous layer. "Now you're ready. Fuck me, Madden. Please, fuck me."

Without further ado he pulls his fingers out and replaces them with the thick tip of his cock. I whimper at the mild burning stretch. But, just like with preparing me, Madden takes his time. He guides me down his length one inch at a time until I'm fully seated and we both let out a breathless moan. I'm still stinging a bit from the invasion but when I give my hips an experimental roll, I see stars behind my eyelids.

"Oh, fuck, that feels good."

Madden nods, fingers digging into my hips as he guides my thrusts.

"So tight."

I lean forward so my hands frame Madden's face and I thrust down again. This time the head of his erection grazes my prostate and I wail with pleasure. I've heard about prostate stimulation, and certainly harnessed it from the other side of the equation. Until this moment I'd never experienced it first-hand.

Pre-cum dribbles from my tip and pools on Madden's stomach as I continue to ride him, probing my prostate with every pass. There's no way I'm going to last much longer, as my balls draw tight and my body starts to tremble with pleasure.

Madden's muscles tighten beneath my hands and he reaches for my erection. Wrapping it in a tight fist he starts to jerk me in time with my thrusts. *Oh god, oh fuck, holy fucking hell that's...unh!*

"I'm coming," I gasp as my ass clenches hard around Madden's cock and liquid heat pulses through my veins. I can't even breathe through the pleasure as my entire body clenches and releases over and over for what feels like an eternity.

"Fuck," Madden cries, thrusting hard into my ass a few times before tensing beneath me with a look of pure ecstasy sweeping over his beautiful face.

Between the look on his face and my release streaking his abs and chest, I'm positive there's no hotter sight in all of human history.

My body finally goes limp, aftershocks subsiding and breathing returning to near normal.

"Holy god, that was…"

"Yeah," Madden agrees as I roll off him and kiss his shoulder. He rolls towards me and nuzzles into my neck with a contented sigh.

"Will you stay?" He asks, his arms flexing around me in an effort to keep me in place. I could laugh out loud at the idea of fucking and running from Madden.

"Of course," I assure him, brushing a kiss against the top of his head.

Madden

I wake up in a cozy cocoon of sleepy happiness. I haven't slept that well in weeks. I'm guessing I owe the good night sleep and full body satisfaction to the phenomenal orgasm. Although, the gorgeous man pressed up against my back might have something to do with it, too. Thane's nose nuzzles against the back of my neck and he lets out a contented sigh and starts to trace little circles on my hipbone with his thumb.

"Morning," I murmur, unwilling to even roll over and ruin this perfect moment.

"Mmmm, good morning," Thane hums, trailing gentle kisses along my shoulder.

At least there's no morning after awkwardness. However, I'm loath to have the 'what does this mean' talk. Maybe we can put it off for a little while.

"Will I be showing my hand too much if I ask what last night means?" Thane asks.

Fuck.

I let out a sigh and force myself to wriggle out of his grasp enough to roll over and face him. I wince as I shuffle around in the bed, putting too much weight briefly on my bad leg. Once I'm settled, I lay my head back on the pillow and take a moment to get lost in Thane's soulful brown eyes.

"I like you a lot," I start and Thane frowns. "No pouty faces. It's not a brush off, I'm stating a fact. I like you a lot."

Thane relaxes a fraction and brings his hand up to cup my jaw, running a thumb through my morning stubble.

"I like you a lot too, Madden."

Now comes the hard part.

"If this were any other circumstances you'd have to have me surgically removed in order to get rid of me. I'd be pulling out all the stops to make you my boyfriend."

"But…?" Thane's expression returns to wariness.

"My head isn't on straight right now. I'm afraid that if we start something right now it'll be doomed before we even start."

Thane sighs and his eyes fill with a sad resignation.

"I know. That's why I hadn't made any moves until now. I knew you weren't in a place for this, yet. Is it too late to dial it back, maybe put this on the backburner until the time is right?"

A warm hopeful feeling fills my chest and tingles down my limbs.

"I'd like that."

Thane closes the small gap between us and brushes a fleeting kiss to my lips, full of promise and longing.

"Alright, I need coffee and food." I can tell Thane's putting on a brave face, and I appreciate it.

My leg is stiff as I ease out of bed, but Thane is there to help me up. It's easy to imagine what it would be like to build a life with a man like Thane. He's the kind of man who'd be there for me through thick and thin. He's husband material. It's just my fucking luck that I'd meet the perfect man when I'm so fucked up in the head that I can't sleep and I'm one bad day away from falling back into a drug addiction I was sure I'd kicked years ago. Why does life have to be such a cruel bitch?

When we reach the kitchen I plop down into a chair while Thane busies himself making coffee and I try not to drool over his well sculpted ass.

I grasp my pencil in my good hand and snap it in half to punish it for refusing to create art. I'm doing my exercises but every time I try to draw a damn thing my hand shakes so badly I can't manage anything remotely legible.

"It's okay to be frustrated," Thane assures me as he enters the room and notices the pencil bits scattered on the coffee table.

"Yeah, is it okay to be a useless, unemployed, loser? Because that's where I'm headed," I bristle. What I wouldn't give for the bitter taste of Oxycontin, crushed between my teeth. I can't tattoo anymore anyway. Maybe I'll never tattoo again. So what's stopping me from finding the pills I gave to Thane to hide?

"You're none of those things. Now, stop throwing yourself a pity party and get back to doing your exercises."

His commanding voice sends a small thrill up my spine, allowing me to forget my pouting and drug-addled fantasies, if only briefly.

"Sir, yes, sir," I tease.

"That's more like it."

My phone buzzes with an incoming text, and Thane passes it to me from its spot on the coffee table.

> **Adam:** hey, feeling up to going out yet? We all miss you at Friday night happy hour
> **Me:** not sure I'm up for that
> **Adam:** Then we'll bring the party to you. See you at ten

"Is it cool if the guys and Dani come by tonight?" I ask Thane, not wanting to be a dick of a houseguest.

"Of course. As long as you're staying here, consider it as much your place as mine. Invite over anyone you like," Thane assures me.

At ten o'clock sharp Adam, Royal, Gage, Nash, and Dani arrive with booze, snacks, and *Cards Against Humanity*.

Hugs and greetings are exchanged as everyone makes themselves right at home in Thane's living room. To his credit, Thane seems happy enough to have my friends there.

I endure the expected several minutes of questions about how I'm feeling, how my physical therapy is going, and questions about why I look so tired. I take it all in stride and quietly assure Adam that I gave my Oxy to Thane so none of them need to worry about that.

I was reluctant to have everyone over, but

now that they're here I feel a little bit more like myself again.

Adam heads into the kitchen and returns with a glass of amber liquid that he hands to me. I take a sip and smile at him.

"Aw, you remembered my favorite drink," I tease him.

"What's your favorite drink?" Thane asks.

"Apple ale with a shot of fire whiskey."

"Apples and cinnamon," Thane mutters quietly, a flash of longing passes behind his dark eyes before he pastes on a smile.

I wonder for the hundredth time today if I made a mistake telling Thane that I'm not ready to start anything. It was true, but fuck if I don't want him. The urge to pull him down on the couch beside me and feel his arm around my shoulders while we hang out with everyone, is almost too much to bear.

I force myself to turn my attention away from Thane and let myself get lost in the familiarity of my best friends. Dani and Gage tease Adam about someone he's apparently been texting a lot who he's refusing to fess up to. Royal shoots longing gazes at Nash whenever Nash turns away from him. And I bask in it all.

Adam and Gage have been best friends since childhood, as have Royal and Nash. So, when I first started at Heathens, I got close with Dani, since the two of us were sort of the odd ones out. But none of the guys ever made us feel like we didn't belong. They pulled us into the fold and acted like they'd known us our whole lives too.

Around eleven o'clock Thane's phone rings and he excuses himself to answer it, that's when the interrogation begins.

"Spill it, you fucked him," Royal accuses with a smile as soon as Thane is out of the room.

"I'm pleading the fifth on this one," I respond, taking a generous gulp of my drink and trying to hide the smirk on my face that would give me away.

"Uh-huh. It's written all over both your faces. He can't stop looking at you like a lost puppy. It's adorable. And every time you think no one's looking, you're undressing him with your eyes."

"Oh, are we going to start discussing the looks people are giving each other when they think no one's looking?"

Royal clams up at my implied threat. While Adam snorts a laugh and Nash's brow furrows in confusion. The distraction only lasts a few second before Adam takes over the line of questioning.

"I'm sure what Royal was trying to say is that we want you to be happy. After that last asshole cheated on you, you deserve a good guy. Thane seems like a really good guy."

"He is a good guy. I'm not in a place for a relationship yet. That's exactly what I told him, and he understood that."

"That's what you told him after you fucked

him, you mean?" Royal jumps in again.

Thane chooses that moment to return to the living room, saving Royal from being throttled.

"Who was calling so late?" I ask.

"A buddy of mine from the marines. He made a last-minute decision not to re-up in two weeks when his tour is up. He was asking if he could come stay here for a little bit while he figures out his next move."

"Oh." That sounds an awful lot like Thane is kicking me out in a few weeks. My leg is getting stronger. I guess I could try to manage stairs. I hadn't realized he'd be so anxious to get rid of me.

"There'll be plenty of room here for both of you, don't worry," he assures me.

We continue to drink and play card games until around two in the morning before everyone decides they'd better head out. Dani had volunteered to be designated driver. I don't envy her as she herds the drunk men into her SUV. Part of me wonders if Royal is playing up the drunk thing a little more than necessary simply to have Nash's steadying arm around him.

Thane

The look of pure happiness on Madden's face makes my heart ache with a yearning to reach out and touch him. It was fun getting to know his friends better, because if things work out down the road, I know how important it will be to get along with his friends. Luckily, I don't have to fake liking them. They're all great people. It's obvious Madden wasn't exaggerating when he'd said Royal was in love with Nash. I felt sort of bad for the guy because he couldn't keep his eyes off his best friend, yet Nash seemed completely oblivious.

I glance at Madden and notice he's dead on his feet. Maybe the alcohol will help him sleep tonight. It's hard not to sweep him up, carry him to his bed, and climb in beside him. Sleep, that's all I want right now, wrapped around Madden in a cozy cocoon.

"Guess I'd better try to sleep," Madden says with a wide yawn. He hesitates and I almost wonder if he's waiting for me to invite myself into his bed. I hesitate too long, and he gives me a tight-lipped smile before turning and making his way down the hall to his room.

CHAPTER 9

Thane

"I need to go somewhere today, can you drive me?" Madden's question catches me off guard as I shuffle into the kitchen in a sleepy stupor. This is the first time in three and a half weeks Madden has *wanted* to leave the house.

"Of course. Where are we going?" I take the mug of steaming coffee he offers me and drop down onto a counter stool.

"Rainbow House."

"The LGBTQ youth center and halfway house?"

"Yeah, the guys and I all volunteer there. We do art classes or just go hang out, let the kids know there are people around who care. I haven't gone in the past few weeks, obviously, and I was thinking this morning that I'm being selfish."

"It's really cool that you guys do that. What got you started?" I ask.

Madden sits down at the kitchen table with his cup of coffee. He looks like he didn't sleep again, which isn't much of a surprise.

"Adam. He's been volunteering there for like six years. Then Gage started going with him.

Royal, Nash, and I started at Heathen around the same time and the next thing you know it was a weekly thing for us all to go," Madden explains.

"Is Adam gay?"

"No, his brother Johnny was. He committed suicide when he was a teenager. He said he never wanted anyone else to feel like there wasn't anyone to talk to."

My respect for Adam grows tenfold, and that's saying something seeing that he saved Madden's life when he was a homeless teen.

"Wow. Now I feel guilty that I've never been down there to volunteer. I might have to make it a regular thing with you."

"Yeah, that'd be cool. Although, you're the last person who should feel guilty about lack of community service. You save lives for a living," Madden points out.

"You can never do too much."

"How are you even real?" Madden jokes, but there's a hint of admiration in his eyes that squeezes my chest.

Madden

In the car on the way to Rainbow House I get myself mentally prepared for a possible panic attack when we arrive. But, as we step inside the familiar building, I feel fine. No racing heart, no shortness of breath. I'm not sure if I'm glad to know there are certain places that I can go without freaking out, or annoyed at myself for freaking out about going benign places like the grocery store.

"You okay?" Thane asks when he notices I've stopped in the entry way.

"Yeah, I'm good," I assure him before leading the way toward reception desk.

Mary, the sweet middle-aged woman who runs the desk glances up. As soon as she sees me her face breaks into a warm smile and she jumps up to come around the desk and greet me. Mary pulls me into a hug that is surprisingly strong for such a petite woman.

"Madden Michael Brody, you had me frightened half to death when I heard you were in the club that night. And then you leave me here for a whole month to worry about how you're doing. I ought to spank your butt."

Did I mention Mary is the mother I never had?

"I'm sorry Mary." I hug her even tighter and give her a kiss on the cheek. "I promise I'm fine, I needed some time to heal before I could make it here, that's all. My hand isn't cooperating just yet, so I'm useless for art classes."

"The kids will understand," Mary assures me. "And, who is this handsome young man?" she asks, noticing Thane behind me for the first time.

Thane steps forward and offers Mary his hand.

"I'm Thane, it's nice to meet you ma'am."

"None of that ma'am stuff. Call me Mary,"

she ignores his outstretched hand and pulls him into a hug as well. I hear a faint 'oomph' as she squeezes the life out of him, and I try to stifle my laugh.

"If you're done crushing Thane's ribcage, mind if we head on back?"

"Of course." Mary waves me in the direction of the double doors that lead to the common area of the house. "I'm betting you'll have a full house back there. We just finished up a mandatory safe sex seminar."

I shoot her a thumbs-up over my shoulder as I head to the back with Thane on my heels.

As soon as I step into the common area all eyes are on me. The air stills for a second as if they're all trying to figure out if I'm a mirage or not. Now I feel even worse for waiting so long to come by. They were all worried about me, and I was holed up feeling sorry for myself.

"This is the greeting I get after a near death experience?" I taunt. That breaks the spell and I'm instantly mobbed by at least fifteen enthusiastic teenagers, all of them asking at the same time how I'm doing, what happened, and why I've been gone so long.

"I'm fine, and the important thing is that I'm here now."

Thane stands back and leaves me to the mob, which takes me several minutes to dissipate.

"Thanks for the help," I say sarcastically.

"You looked like you had it handled," Thane

assures me with a smile. His eyes linger for a few seconds too long, and not in a sexy way. He's making sure I'm not freaking out. Great, I'm officially a mentally fragile person who needs to be watched. Fan-fucking-tastic.

Once everything starts to settle down, I notice a younger looking boy sitting by himself in the bay window.

I glance around until I see one of the aids and motion her over. Lisa is in her thirties and is full of energy. She works hard for the kids at Rainbow House, even though the pay is miniscule and the hours suck. The world could use a thousand more Lisa's.

"Hey, Madden, good to see you." She hugs me like Mary had- that is to say, way too tight.

"You too. Sorry I took so long to get over here after the...uh...incident."

"Oh please, you needed time to heal. Don't let anyone make you feel guilty about that."

"Thanks. Hey, what's up with that kid?" I ask, discreetly motioning towards the boy in the window.

"That's Kyle, his dad kicked him out. He said he saw the flyer for Rainbow House at the coffee shop down the street," Lisa explains.

"He looks young."

"He says he's twelve. That's really all he's told us aside from his name. Wouldn't say why his dad kicked him out, or if there'd been abuse. We asked if he had any other relatives he might want to contact, but he's not giving us anything."

"Cool if I talk to him?"

"Of course."

I let Thane know I'm going to go talk to Kyle and then make my way over to the boy in the window.

"Hey, mind if I sit?" I ask, gesturing to the open space beside him. Kyle pulls his gaze from the window and eyes me wearily, but nods. I sit down and look out the window as well, giving him the chance to start the conversation if he wants to.

"Cool tattoos." *Bingo.*

"Thanks. I'm a tattoo artist."

"Really?" His eyes go wide, and he leans forward to look at my ink a little closer.

"Yeah. I've been an artist my whole life, helped me through a lot of dark times. When I was fourteen my parents kicked me out. I lived on the street for four years before someone took a chance on giving me a job and a place to live. That's when I learned to tattoo and got the chance to change my life," I confide.

"Your parents kicked you out too?"

"Yeah, they didn't like that I was gay," I explain.

Kyle turns his attention back to the window for a few minutes, but the emotions playing across his face make it clear he's trying to get up the courage to open up.

"My dad kicked me out because he caught me trying on a skirt. He said boys can't wear skirts," he admits.

"Now that's just not true. Boys can wear anything they like. Girls can too."

Kyle nods and chews his bottom lip.

"If I like to wear skirts does that mean I'm gay?"

"Not at all."

"My dad said it does."

"How old are you?"

"Twelve."

"Perfect, that's a great age to learn a very important life lesson. Are you ready?" He nods eagerly and sits forward like I'm about to divulge the secret of the universe. "The truth is, life is way more complicated than that."

"It is?"

"Sure. You could be a boy who likes to wear skirts but still likes girls. Or, you could like boys, or maybe both. You could also be a boy who feels like he's supposed to be a girl. And if you are really a girl you could still like boys, girls, or both. Or, you could be a straight boy who was just curious about what wearing a skirt felt like."

"Wow. That's a lot. How will I know which it is?"

"You'll know. It might be hard right now because you're confused by the way your dad says you should be, and the way you think your friends or society expect you to be. But once you do some soul searching and ask yourself what feels right, you'll just know."

He tackles me in a hug and I get the impression he might be trying to hide tears.

"Thank you."

"Anytime, bud. And don't be afraid to talk with or ask questions of anyone who works or volunteers here. We're here to help you. We don't judge."

Thane

I watch as Madden talks to the boy in the window, and a strange sense of admiration comes over me. I can't hear what's being said, but the gentle expression on Madden's face, and the awed look in the boy's eyes lets me know that he's getting through to him.

"Madden, are you going to do an art lesson today?" one of the older boys calls out from across the room.

"Sorry, dude, my hand is out of commission. Hopefully next time."

The boy's face falls and I can tell Madden is considering for a second giving it a try with his hand.

"How about if I teach you guys some cool stuff I learned in the marines?" I offer. All eyes are on me now, with varying degrees of excitement.

"Can you teach me how to kill a man with one finger?"

"No. But I can teach you how to get out of a choke hold,"

"Awesome!"

Two hours later we're climbing back into my car, exhausted.

"Damn, those kids have energy."

"What's the matter old man, can't keep up with teenagers anymore?" Madden teases.

"I *am* pushing thirty," I agree with mock seriousness.

"Damn, you're going to have grey pubes any day now," he taunts.

"Watch it, twenty-three turns to twenty-nine in the blink of an eye," I warn. "You hungry?"

"Starving."

"Burgers?" I suggest. Madden hesitates but then smiles and nods after a few seconds.

Over the next few minutes Madden goes from joking and relaxed to tense and quiet. I'm tempted to suggest that I just run in and grab the burgers and we can head home. But I also don't want to coddle him. If Madden can't handle something, he can tell me, he's an adult after all.

I pull up in front of the small burger place and get out of the car. Madden isn't far behind, but he looks like he's on his way to his execution rather than dinner.

We step inside and Madden's body is strung so taut I swear I could play him like a guitar string. I place a comforting hand on his lower back, but he seems to be lost in his own world. His eyes are glazed over, his breaths coming in short pants, and his entire body is trembling.

"Madden, it's okay. I'm here, everything is okay." I step close, pulling him into my arms to soothe him. He relaxes a fraction and lets out a quiet sob.

"I need to go, please, can we go?"

"Of course." Ignoring the sideways glances we're getting from other patrons and wait staff I steer Madden back out the door and towards the car.

It takes another five minutes of driving before Madden's breathing returns to normal and his body starts to relax.

"I'm sorry," he says in almost a whisper as we near the house.

"It's okay. We can order takeout or something. I'm more worried about how you're doing than about dinner. What happened?"

"I don't want to talk about it. I'm fine now." Madden's tone holds an air of finality.

I itch to push him, to demand to know where his head's at and what I can do to help. On the other hand, I don't want to drive him away. I want him to feel comfortable coming to me when he's ready. I'm sure he needs more time to process and move forward.

Madden

I can't believe what an idiot I made of myself at the burger place. It was the first almost date-like thing Thane and I were doing together, and I went and fucked it up. I started getting anxious as soon as he'd suggested it. But I'd done so well at Rainbow House I figured all the panic attack stuff was all in my head, that I was blowing it out of proportion.

I told myself I would face the fear and be fine. I spent the next few minutes in the car giving myself a mental pep talk. The second I set foot in the unfamiliar setting, with all those strangers, my brain short circuited. I couldn't see anything except for memories of the night at the club. I was trapped in a nightmare that I couldn't escape.

It was a godsend when Thane's warm embrace pulled me back from the dark.

I should explain to Thane what happened. I should be up front about the panic attacks, the flashbacks. But fuck if it isn't embarrassing. He was there that night and he's sleeping like a baby. Hell, he's been god knows where and seen god knows what with the marines. Thane literally runs into burning buildings for a living. He's fine. He can handle all of it. So, why am I so mentally weak? Why am I only seconds away from a complete breakdown?

"That was fun today, at Rainbow House," Thane says, breaking my thoughts and joining me on the couch. He must've finished ordering whatever he decided on for dinner. I'd told him I didn't have a preference and he could order whatever.

"Yeah, they're good kids. I'm glad there's a

place for them to go. I wish I'd known about places like that back in the day."

"You're good with those kids, they're lucky to have you."

Thane's words are like a balm to my soul. All I've ever wanted is to save someone else from what I went through. If I can spare just one kid from the feelings of rejection and hopelessness I suffered I'll die happy. I had Adam to pull me out of the darkness, and I want to be that for someone else. I swallow around the lump in my throat and nod at his comment, unable to speak.

"You want kids someday?" Thane asks. His tone is impassive, but the question feels loaded. We agreed now is not the time for us to pursue anything, but maybe one day...

"Yeah. I always thought I'd like to foster one or two kids like the ones at Rainbow house. And... I don't know...littler kids are pretty cool too..." I stammer out my answer, feeling heat creeping into my cheeks. Thane gives me a shy smile, something lingering behind his eyes that I can't quite place.

"Me too," he agrees.

The air hangs heavy between us until I scoot forward and lay my head on his shoulder. Thane doesn't hesitate to wrap his arm around me and hold me close. If I can get my head on straight this might just be close to perfect.

CHAPTER 10

Thane

Standing in front of the airport I lean against my car and wait for my buddy. I haven't seen Zade since I left the Marines four years ago. Zade and I were close back in the day. More than close, actually. Not that it was ever anything serious, just a way for us both to scratch an itch while deployed without blowing our covers as gay men.

"Well if it isn't the Kraken," a smile spreads across my face as I hear Zade's voice. I turn and spot him coming toward me.

"Zade!" I push myself off the car and meet him halfway, wrapping him in a hug and giving him a firm clap on the back. "It's fucking good to see you, man."

"Likewise." I pop my trunk open and Zade tosses his bags in before making his way around to the passenger side.

"Thanks for letting me crash with you for a few days," he says as I jump into the car and pull away from the curb.

"No problem. Brother's for life, right?" I offer my fist for a bump which Zade returns.

"I hope not too brotherly," Zade's voice

takes on a deeper timbre and my stomach knots. *Oh shit, this just got awkward.*

"Um, about that…" I risk a quick glance at him before I ease onto the on ramp for the highway. "I'm seeing someone. Well, not actually seeing him, but I want to be seeing him. He's staying with me right now. I should've said something sooner. I'm sorry if I made things weird."

Zade is quiet for several seconds before he gives me a friendly slug to my arm and lets out a laugh.

"Dude, I'm the one who just made things weird. Okay, we're going to pretend *that* never happened and you're going to tell me all about your man. What's his name? How'd you meet?"

I let out a relieved breath.

"His name is Madden, and we met last month. It's the worst ever 'how we met' story, to be honest. We met at a nightclub and before I could work up the game to take him home with me, there was a shooting. He was shot three times."

"Holy fuck."

"Yeah, it was crazy. He's okay now, or getting there anyway. He's staying with me while he recovers because his place was a fifth-floor walkup, and he's got a bum leg now."

"So, not dating but you want to be?"

"Yeah," I let out a wistful sigh.

"You've slept with him, though," Zade says knowingly.

"Only once. He's still healing physically and emotionally so I didn't want to push him, and he said he wasn't ready for anything right now," I explain.

"I'm sure he'll come around, you're a great guy."

I don't miss the longing tone in his voice, so I scramble to change the subject.

"So, are you going to tell me why you didn't re-up? I was sure you were a lifer."

"I thought so too, but...things change." Zade's tone is more subdued than I've ever heard it before.

"Do you want to talk about it?" I offer.

"Not so much. Maybe later."

"Okay, I'm here any time you need to talk."

"Not re-enlisting is starting to feel like a big fucking mistake. Now I don't know what I'm going to do with my goddamn life."

"That's pretty much where I was at when I left, too. You'll figure it out. And, until then you'll take my bed and I'm sleeping on the couch."

"No way, I'll sleep on the couch," Zade argues.

"My house, my rules. I'm sleeping on the couch."

Zade laughs.

"Alright. Thanks, man."

"Anytime, you know that."

Zade lets out a low whistle when we pull up in front of my house.

"This place is nice."

"I like it," I agree with a chuckle.

When we get inside, I find Madden on the couch watching *Tattoo Nightmares* and doing his hand exercises. On the table are a few pieces of paper with semi-legible sketches on them, and pencils that are not broken. It's an improvement.

He looks up and smiles at me. My heart stutters at the way his gaze rakes over my body before he schools his features and turns his attention to Zade.

"Hi, you must be Zade." He offers a hand to shake and Zade takes it with a friendly smile.

"I am. I'm assuming you're Madden, unless Thane is keeping a whole mess of guys at his house."

"Nope, just me," Madden assures him with a laugh.

"How about I grill up some steaks for dinner?" I suggest as Zade settles into the chair beside the couch.

They both agree and then start chatting about Madden's job and Zade's plans now that he's out of the Marines.

Madden

Zade seems like a cool guy. While Thane

127

cooked dinner Zade and I chatted, and I decided I liked him. Then I noticed his eyes lingering on Thane's ass when Thane brought beers into the living room. When Zade thought neither of us would notice his gaze roamed all over Thane's body with a familiarity that made my skin crawl. It wasn't the lecherous look of someone dying to know how someone else looks naked. It was the intimate and longing look of someone who's already seen the other person naked.

Then it occurs to me that maybe that's why Thane brought him here. I told him I wasn't in a place for a relationship, he has every right to move on and find someone else. Flames of jealousy lick at my skin. If I wasn't a damn cripple right now, I'd hoist Thane over my shoulder, take him to the bedroom, and fuck him until he forgot that other men even existed in the world.

"Madden?" Thane's voice pulls me from my jealous fantasy.

"Huh?"

"I asked if Zade could tag along to Rainbow House next time we go," Thane repeats the question he apparently already asked me.

"Uh, yeah, sure." I agree. The kids thought Thane was super cool, being a marine and a firefighter. I'm sure they'll be crazy about Zade as well.

The rest of the evening is spent eating a delicious dinner and then playing a few hands of poker. Around ten Zade stands up from the table and stretches, exposing miles of chiseled muscles on his abdomen. Stupid, ripped marine.

"I'm pretty beat, think I'm going to head to bed," Zade announces.

My stomach knots as he heads up the stairs to Thane's bedroom. I guess that answers that question. They are sleeping together. Zade will be in Thane's bed night after night, while I lay down here and beat myself up for not snatching up Thane when I had the chance.

"You tired or you want to do an episode of S.O.A. before bed?"

"Is that even a question?" I laugh. Anything to keep Thane with me instead of up in bed with Zade.

I follow Thane out of the kitchen and into the living room. I'm already stronger on my leg with a few weeks of PT, and my hand is getting better little by little. Now if only I could get past the nightmares I'd be in good shape.

Thane drops down on the couch, leaving very little room for me, forcing me to press up against him. One of his strong arms comes down around my shoulders and I relax against his chest. Every ounce of jealousy that had been tormenting me all day bubbles to the surfaces as the heat of Thane's body washes over me. Before the rational part of my brain has a chance to add its two-cents I'm on him.

My lips attack Thane's, hot and demanding. My tongue flicks against the seam of his lips, requesting entrance, and Thane grants it readily. His fingers wind into my hair and tug me closer, urging me to deepen the kiss. He moans into my mouth as I climb onto his lap, blanketing his body with my own. Thane is mine, I'm not letting Zade— or anyone else— have him.

I thrust my hips, grinding my erection against his through our jeans. Flames of desire blaze in my gut, demanding more.

Thane whimpers as I snake one hand between us and start unfastening his jeans.

"Madden," he gasps tugging my bottom lip between his teeth and making quick work of my pants as well.

"Tell me you're mine," I beg as I trail kisses along his jaw and down the column of his neck.

"I'm yours," Thane pants, shoving my pants down my hips and then lifting his own lower body off the couch so I can shove his pants down as well. Lust punches me in the gut as I take in the sight of Thane breathless beneath me, his hard, dripping cock inches from my own.

When my eyes land on his kiss swollen lips, every cell in my body compels me to lean in for another taste, and I don't bother to resist. I sink forward, pressing our heated erections together as our lips meet again in a frenzied kiss. This time when I thrust my hips forward I'm blessed with the friction of skin on skin, rather than clothing between us. Thane gasps into my mouth and grinds against me, our combined pre-cum slicking the way for our fevered frotting.

Thane's hands are everywhere, sparking electric currents across my skin everywhere they land. At some point we shed our shirts, I couldn't for the life of me say when. One of Thane's thumbs grazes my peaked nipple and I whimper against his mouth and pump my hips faster, harder, chasing the blind need coursing through my veins.

"So good. Fuck, you're so hot," I moan against Thane's lips. His fingers dig in to the globes of my ass, urging me on until he's writing beneath me, arching his back and murmuring incoherently. The feeling of his cock pulsing against mine, cum coating both of us, is enough to send me careening over the edge into my own orgasm.

"Fuck, yeah, oh god I'm coming," I moan into the side of his neck as I get lost in pleasure.

I collapse against him, not even caring that we're both covered in jizz and sweat.

"Not that I'm complaining, *at all*, but what the hell was that?" Thane asks, still breathing heavily.

"Fuck, sorry, I'm sending mixed signals, aren't I?"

"Little bit, yeah."

I wince and bury my face against Thane's bare chest, allowing myself to get drunk on his scent for just a few seconds.

"It's stupid. I guess I got jealous of you and Zade. Fuck, I ruined things for you guys, didn't I?"

"Me and Zade?" Thane's brows knit together

in confusion.

"Yeah, I get it. I told you I wasn't ready, you had every right to reconcile with an old boyfriend, or whatever Zade is." The words taste bitter on my tongue. I know I should be diplomatic, but I want Thane to myself.

"I'm not with Zade," Thane says, and I let out a relieved sigh.

"Really? He's sleeping in your bed."

"And I'm sleeping on the couch or in your bed if you invite me."

The knot in my chest that's been pulling tighter and tighter since I first saw Zade check Thane out, finally eases.

"Then let's go lay down in bed and talk," I suggest.

We walk down the hallway, leaving our clothes in the living room, and make a quick pit stop in the bathroom to get cleaned up. Then we slip into my bed and Thane pulls me close, just like he did the other night.

"I like you a lot," I admit, idly running my hand along his chest. "But, I'm still not..."

"Shh," Thane silences me with a peck on the lips. "I already told you that you've got me right where you want me," he jokes. "I understand the need to take things slow, so let's keep it casual, call it fun for now, and not stress about it."

"Okay," I agree, ready to say yes to anything that will allow me to have Thane in my bed again. "Exclusive though, right?"

"Absolutely."

"So, you and Zade never...?" I almost don't want to know, but I can't have been imagining the way Zade was looking at him.

When Thane is silent longer than expected I tilt my head to look at his face. I find him blushing and giving me an apologetic look.

"It was years ago, and it never meant any- thing. I told him as soon as he got here that I only wanted you now and he completely understood."

"I doubt he *completely* understood. He was looking at you like he wanted to suck your soul out through your cock."

"Madden, no one is sucking my cock but you until you tell me to get lost. Okay?"

"Okay." I snuggle close and let the soothing rhythm of his heart beat lull me to sleep.

The feeling of warm lips against my shoul- der startles me awake.

"It's just me, didn't mean to scare you." Thane soothes me with another kiss between my shoulder blades. His usually deep voice even more rough from sleep sets a fire in the pit of my stom- ach. I make a move to roll over so I can kiss him, but his hand pushes firmly against the middle of my back, keeping me on my stomach, in the pos- ition I woke up in.

"Don't you dare move."

Thane's hot breath tickles the back of my

neck, sending a shiver down my spine. Then his morning wood brushes against my lower back and I moan into my pillow. His lips continue their journey across my shoulders and slowly down my spine. I flex my hips, grinding my erection against the smooth sheets and let out another moan.

Thane's strong hands grasp the globes of my ass and kneads them. I thrust again reflexively, chasing the pleasure Thane's bestowing on me. His next kiss lands on my lower back, just above my ass. And then— because apparently there is a god who does in fact love gays—his tongue begins to lavish my crack, making his way to my hole.

"Oh fuck," I gasp, my hands fisting my pillow.

When the flat of his tongue strokes the sensitive bundle of nerves around my asshole, I let out a string of curses and prayers to every deity I can think of.

He moans appreciatively, shoving his greedy tongue inside me.

I'm harder than I've been in my entire life as I grind against the bed, creating a substantial wet spot.

"Oh god, oh fuck. Thane, *god.*"

"Just Thane is fine," he murmurs playfully before continuing his task.

"Fuck me, Thane. Please."

"Is your leg okay in this position?" He asks, replacing his tongue with his index finger, circling my tight entrance.

"Yeah, I'm fine," I insist, using my good leg to propel myself to thrust against his finger, trying to encourage him to fuck me with it.

"You'll tell me if at any point there's pain or discomfort in your leg." His tone is firm, commanding, and hot as fuck. Finally, he eases his finger inside of me and I whimper, biting down on my pillow.

Luckily, Thane brought more than one condom down with him last time. Was it really only two weeks ago? Ever the multitasker he adds a second finger, while reaching forward with his free hand to grab the condom and lube from the top of the nightstand. I wince as he drizzles some cold lube between my ass cheeks.

"Sorry," he mutters, pulling his fingers out and using them to spread the lube around, warming it in the process. The sound of a wrapper tearing reaches my ears and I thrust back again, desperate to have Thane stretching me, owning me.

Moments later the thick head of his cock is pressing against my entrance.

"Okay?" He asks, voice tight with restraint.

"Yes, fuck, yes."

I suck in a breath at the sharp sting of his first thrust. He stills, buried deep in my ass, and leans forward to blanket my body with his.

"I've got you baby." he assures me, trailing light kisses along the shell of my ear.

"Thane, please," I gasp, desperate for him to move inside me.

He understands my plea and withdraws until he pulls almost all the way out, before thrusting deep again, hitting my prostate on the way back in. I let out a strangled cry of approval. He repeats the motion, pistoning his hips fast and hard, making me see stars with every thrust. Heat builds inside me as my balls draw tight. My body starts to quake with waves of pleasure pulsing through me.

"Oh god, I'm gonna…unh!"

My bliss spills over, euphoria bursting from every cell in my body. I vaguely register the feeling of Thane's orgasm pulsing through his cock and it adds to my own arousal.

When he collapses on top of me I'm thoroughly spent and utterly satisfied.

After a few seconds he rolls off me and I'm left feeling cold.

"Are you okay?" He asks, running a hand up and down my spine, as he tries to catch his breath.

"I'm fantastic," I answer and then roll onto my side to get out of the mess I created. "Think I'm going to have to wash the sheets today."

Thane glances over my shoulder and laughs.

"Yeah, that's a lot of cum. Damn, that's really fucking hot. You know, you're way more of a cock slut than you let on."

"Oh my god, shut up," I laugh and playfully shove him away from me, but Thane hangs on tight kissing and biting the back of my neck as we tussle.

"Come on, let's get some breakfast." Thane gives my ass a hard smack that causes me to yelp, and then climbs out of bed.

"Dick," I mutter, rubbing my stinging ass.

"Oh please, you liked it," Thane teases.

I ease out of bed noticing the difference a good night sleep makes on the aching in my body. Six weeks of rehab and my leg is doing well. I've got an appointment for a follow-up x-ray this week so the doctor can tell me if the fracture is healed. I'm not all that worried about it. It was my hand that had me worried, and it's coming along. Although, not as quickly as I would've liked. My PT keeps telling me to keep at it and not get discouraged. I can't stop wondering what I'll do if I can never draw the same again? If I can't hold a tattoo gun, what the fuck am I going to do?

CHAPTER 11

Madden

It's more awkward than I expected it to be when Thane leaves for work and I'm left alone with Zade. Knowing that Thane didn't invite him here to rekindle an old relationship helps. I can't ignore the furtive looks he continued to throw Thane over breakfast.

"Any plans for today?" Zade asks.

"Aside from doing my exercises, no."

"Cool. Listen, I'm dying for some new ink. Can you recommend someone for me?"

I perk up at this question. Is it too shameless of me to throw him at my slutty friend? *Nah.*

"Oh yeah, my buddy Royal does great work. All the guys do, but I think Royal is the man you want." *In more ways than one, hopefully.* "We can head over there if you want, I'm sure he'll make time for you."

"Awesome. Let me shower and stuff and then I'm up for it any time."

Pushing open the door to Heathen Ink a

wave of homesickness washes over me. I flex my hand instinctively, wondering if I'll get full use back or not.

The panic I've felt in public recently is nowhere to be found as I enter the shop, for which I'm eternally grateful. This is my second home.

"Mad Dog," Dani jumps off the stool behind the front counter and races toward me. I tense, bracing for impact. Luckily, she pulls up short at the last minute and manages to give me a hug that doesn't knock me on my ass. I wrap my arms around her and crush her dainty body against me.

"Hey, sweetheart. How's it going?"

"Good, slow day." She gestures to the empty shop.

"Perfect. Is Royal free?" I ask, and then gesture to Zade who's trailing behind me. "Thane's buddy wants some ink, I thought Royal would be the man for the job."

Dani's brows furrow, but then she looks Zade over and understanding dawns in her eyes. She shoots me a look that tells me that I am, in fact, as shameless as I suspected I might be. Sorry, not sorry.

"Yeah, he's free. He's sketching back in his area."

"Great. You free to give me some quick ink too?"

"Yeah, go get Zade settled and come find me."

I nod and then gesture for Zade to follow me

towards the back of the shop. I peek around the wall that separates Royal's area from the front of the shop and find him in his chair with his sketch book in his lap, just as Dani said he'd be.

"Hey, Royal."

"Oh, hey man." He glances up, seemingly surprised to see me. "What brings you by?"

"This is Thane's buddy, Zade. He wants a tat."

Royal glances past me and notices Zade for the first time. His expression goes from curious to heated in seconds flat.

"Why, hello there. Why don't you step on in here and tell me what I can do for you, sexy."

"Alright, I'll leave you in Royal's very capable hands." I pat Zade on the shoulder and notice he's gifting Royal with a look that can only be described as smoldering. *Thank you, baby Jesus.*

I make my way back toward the front of the shop to find Dani.

"Ready?" I ask her.

"Of course." She waves me into her alcove and starts pulling out her equipment. "What do you want?"

I yank my shirt over my head and settle into her chair. I point towards the scar just below my ribcage.

"I want 'Bullet Proof' right over the scar."

Dani gives me a disapproving look at my sardonic request.

"Seriously?"

"Yeah. Please?"

She lets out a long-suffering sigh but continues to prep without further comment.

I lay back and enjoy the familiar burn of needle biting into skin. Who needs therapy when you can get inked?

"So, how are things?" Dani asks as she works.

"Better now that I've pawned off Captain do-me eyes on Royal."

Dani snorts a laugh and shakes her head at me.

"I take it there's more than friendship between Zade and Thane?"

"Not if I have anything to say about it," I bluster, feeling the hot surge of jealousy course through me again at the thought.

"Ooo, someone's going all alpha male," Dani teases.

"Hardly," I roll my eyes at her. "I'm not about to give up Thane without a fight."

"Based on the way he was looking at you the other night when we were all over, I don't think you have anything to worry about."

Her words bring a smile to my face. Thane is amazing, generous, a truly good man. And he wants *me*. Now if I can find a way to be worthy of that affection we'll be all set.

"Hey man, didn't know you were here," Adam peeks his head into Dani's workspace and looks over the ink she's giving me. He shakes his head and then laughs at my ironic choice of tattoo.

"All done," Dani declares, giving a final wipe to the area and then swiping on some Aquapor ointment.

"I just made coffee, want some?" Adam offers.

"Yeah," I agree, following him to the break room in the back of the shop.

"You look like you're getting around a lot better," Adam notes.

"Yeah, getting the follow-up x-ray tomorrow, but I think my leg is pretty well healed. Now I just need to get my hand back in shape. The muscles are getting there, but the nerve damage..." I didn't want to believe my PT when he told me I might forever have a tremor in my right hand. You can't tattoo if you've got the shakes like someone who's detoxing.

Thane

"Mmmm, something smells good," I sniff the air as I walk into the kitchen. Walking up behind Madden I slide my arms around him from behind and nuzzle the back of his neck while he stirs whatever he's cooking.

"We have the house to ourselves tonight, so I thought I'd make you dinner," Madden says grinding that perky ass against my growing arousal.

"Where'd Zade go?"

"Out with Royal," he says with a hint of smug satisfaction.

"Did you set that up?"

"Not really. I introduced them, that was all."

"Now that I'm thinking about it, they make a pretty good match." I sneak a hand under his t-shirt and tease my fingers along the ridge of his abs, tracing from his belly button and down his happy trail until he shivers. "I've been thinking about you all day."

"That makes two of us."

Reaching forward, Madden turns off the burner and then turns in my arms so we're nose to nose, foreheads together, sharing breath.

Undeterred from my journey down his happy trail I cup his erection through his sweatpants. He groans and bucks his hips forward.

"Mmmm, need something, baby?" I taunt, tightening my grip and running my tongue from his ear to his jaw.

"I need you to stop teasing and suck my dick." Madden punctuates his demand by grabbing my hair.

"God I love it when you're bossy," I moan, giving his neck a quick nip before dropping to my knees in front of him. I make quick work of his pants, eager to have his gorgeous cock in my face and in my mouth, in that order.

With his pants around his ankles Madden sways on his feet, I grab his thighs to steady him. Burying my nose in the juncture between his balls and his thigh I inhale deeply, getting drunk on his scent. Then, I turn my head to the side and flick my tongue along the seam of his balls until he's panting and tugging my hair between his fingers. The man has no patience. I refuse to be rushed. I nudge his legs apart, forcing him to lean back against the counter, and I continue my oral exploration by licking the tender skin between his balls and ass.

Madden lets out a frustrated grunt, reaching for his leaking cock, but I slap his hand away and continue my leisurely pace.

When my tongue brushes against his puckered hole he lets out a string of curses. God I love turning this man to putty in my hands- or in this case my mouth.

"Please, Thane," he pleads and whimpers, thrusting his throbbing dick in search of relief.

Having mercy on him I finally lick my way up the underside of his erection, circle the salty head, and then swallow him down greedily. He's almost too much to take all the way in, but I do love the challenge. My balls ache as I slurp and suck Madden with a hungry vigor. Reaching up I gently tug and massage his balls as they draw tight against his body.

"God, fuck, yes, christ." Madden rambles incoherently.

He swells and stiffens even further in my mouth, and I know he's about to blow. I relax my throat and swallow around the swollen head and he lets out a loud cry, thrusting against my face as he empties himself into my mouth.

I take every drop he gives me and then lick

him clean when he's done to make sure I haven't missed an ounce of his delicious cum. He shudders as my tongue passes a final time over the sensitive head of his cock. I tuck him back into his pants and stand to pull him into a slow, leisurely kiss.

"Alright, food, let's do this," I say, giving Madden a playful smack on the ass and then assessing the cooking situation he has going on.

"Not much else to do at the moment. I'm making chili so it just has to sit for a while and then we can eat. Beer?"

I wave him off and grab a couple of beers from the fridge for us. Once I twist the caps off and pass one to Madden, I take a sip and a goofy smile spreads across my face.

"Want to know what I do when I cook by myself?"

Madden raises an eyebrow at me, as he waits to hear the answer. I lean in like I'm going to tell him a secret and instead I bust out into a falsetto rendition of 'Call Me Maybe'. Madden laughs so I go for broke, throwing my arms in the air and wiggling my ass around like a fifteen-year-old girl at a pop concert.

When Madden doubles over in hysterics I grab him around the waist and force him to dance with me.

"You're a really good guy, Thane. You sure you want anything to do with my crazy ass?" He says it like a joke, but the way his eyebrows crease I know his worry is genuine.

"Madden," I stop dancing and put a finger under his chin to tilt his face towards mine. "I'm crazy about you. Got it?"

He bites his lip against a smile and nods before crashing his lips into mine.

"I need a shower."

"Is that an invitation?" Madden teases.

"Babe, consider yourself invited to shower with me times infinity."

Madden

I don't know why Thane likes me, but I'm not about to look a gift horse in the mouth. Especially when I've got my hands all over his slippery, wet body. He relaxes into my touch as I soap him up, making sure not to miss a single square inch.

"Did you get this tattoo today?" Thane asks, tracing my new *Bullet Proof* tattoo.

"Yeah, Dani did it for me."

"It's a bit cheeky, but I like it."

"Glad to have your seal of approval," I reply sarcastically before turning Thane around and running my soapy hands along his back.

When my soap-slicked hands find their way around his waist and to his substantial erection Thane moans and bucks his hips.

"Anyone ever tell you that you've got an amazing cock?" I ask as I jerk him nice and slow.

"Other people exist?" he teases in a choked voice as my free hand finds his balls and gives them a gentle tug. "Jesus, yeah, just like that."

Thane thrusts into my hand and I take mercy on him and jerk his cock faster, harder until he starts to tense against me. My lips and teeth find his neck and I shamelessly mark him as his release coats my hand before the warm spray from the shower washes it away. Thane continues to twitch and thrust until his orgasm passes, then he leans his head against my shoulder, breathing heavy.

"Best shower ever."

CHAPTER 12

Madden

After Thane leaves for work the following day I spend most of the morning doing my exercises and getting annoyed as hell when my hand continues to tremor too severely to draw anything, and doing my best not to wonder if Thane ever did flush my Oxy.

When Zade returns home in the afternoon he has a dark, purple hickey on his neck and I do an internal happy dance.

"Good date with Royal?"

Zade smile and drops down on the couch beside me.

"*Good* is an understatement. Your friend is a freak, dude."

"Eww, no details please. I do not need to know what Royal gets up to in bed. It's bad enough to picture him and Nash tag teaming girls together." I shake my head against the image. Then I notice Zade frowning at me. "Oh shit, forget I said that."

It's common knowledge among our group of friends that Royal and Nash have a habit of bringing girls home for some three-way action.

My stupid brain forgot to filter my mouth, though. Of course Royal wouldn't tell a guy on the first date that he tag team's girls with his straight best friend, duh.

"Not something that's easy to forget. Don't worry, it's not a problem for me. I was just surprised, that's all."

"Okay, sorry, I shouldn't have said that. Please don't tell Royal I said anything?"

Zade waves me off with assurances that he won't say anything.

"I was thinking of stopping by to see Thane at work, you want to come?" Zade offers.

As if on cue, the moment the idea of going out somewhere unfamiliar is presented my lungs seize and my body tenses.

"We shouldn't bother him at work," I argue.

"I asked him before, and he said that unless they're out on a call it's boring. They sit around and wait for stuff to happen. So, you want to come?"

My heart pounds and I try to hide the fact that my lungs refuse to expand adequately.

"No, thanks," I hurry to stand up and make my way down the hall to my bedroom before Zade can say anything else.

Thane

"Hey, Thane, you've got a visitor," Hayden calls out from the first floor of the firehouse. Who the hell would be visiting me at work? I finish wiping down the kitchen table and head downstairs to see who's there.

"Hope I'm not bugging you. Just thought I'd stop by and see your station," Zade says, glancing around at the garage area. His eyes linger on Hayden, washing the truck for a moment and I pin him with a 'keep dreaming, he's straight' glare.

"You're not bugging me. Truth be told, it gets pretty boring sitting around here waiting for an emergency to happen. Come on up, I'll show you around and you can hang out for a bit if you want."

Zade follows me back up the stairs and I introduce him to the guys who are hanging out in the common area. When I get to Brad, Zade receives a derisive snort.

"This your boyfriend?" Brad sneers. Zade stiffens beside me before a wolfish grin appears on his lips.

"Why, you interested? You look like a real power bottom, am I right?" Zade taunts him. Brad's face goes bright red and his eyes narrow at Zade.

"Don't talk to me like that you disgusting faggot," Brad bites out.

"Problem in here boys?" The captain barks as he enters the room in time to hear Brad's slur. "Brad, why don't you come with me for a little chat?"

"Sir, you can't possibly be alright with Thane bringing his boyfriend here to fuck during his shift," Brad challenges.

"Captain, this isn't my boyfriend. This is my buddy from the marines, Zade," I introduce him.

The captain offers Zade a hand to shake and then eyes him up with speculation.

"Looking to become a firefighter?"

"I'm not sure, sir. Still working on figuring out my next step."

"Well, if you make a decision come see me. I like having former military on my team."

"Yes sir," Zade nods and gives him a grateful smile.

Brad huffs and crosses his arms over his chest. Guess that didn't go how he hoped it would. Captain pins Brad with a warning look and gestures toward his office for Brad to follow.

After that things settle down and I offer Zade something to drink in the kitchen area.

"That guy was a real dick, huh?" Zade notes. I shrug and pour him a glass of iced tea.

"Yeah, but all the other guys have been cool so it's par for the course."

Zade nods in understanding and then gets quiet. His gaze lingers on his drink, but it's clear from his expression that there's something on his mind.

"So, you and Royal?" I ask.

Zade smiles and his eyes get dreamy.

"Mmmm, yeah, Royal." The pitch of his voice deepens when he says Royal's name, and the look in his eyes tells me all I need to know.

"That good, huh?" I laugh.

"I'm not jinxing anything. New subject."

"Alright, why don't you tell me whatever's on your mind then?" I suggest, since he rejected my gift of a topic change.

"I invited Madden to stop by and visit, too," Zade hedges. "He got kind of wiggy." I bristle at Zade's words, ready to jump to Madden's defense. But he puts up a hand to stop me. "I've known guys with PTSD. A lot of guys, in fact. And, I'm worried about your man."

"He's fine. It's taking him some time to cope with everything that happened. It doesn't help that he can't do his art. You know how artists are, if they can't express themselves, they get all twitchy."

"Are you sure that's all it is?" Zade challenges.

"Yes," I bite out.

"Are you willing to bet his life on it?"

I stiffen, his words cutting to the core and injecting icy fear into my veins. I swallow, unable to answer his question. Of course, I'm not willing to bet Madden's life on it. Ultimately, it's not my call. I can't make Madden go to therapy. When I suggested it he all but bit my head off.

"He's fine," I insist with a lot less vehemence this time.

Zade bites down on his lower lip, his eyes dark with concern. But, he doesn't argue further, just nods his head in acceptance and leans back in the chair.

Madden

I wake with a warm body wrapped around me from behind, and a smile creeps over my face. For the past two weeks since Thane and I decided to give this a try, albeit on a casual basis, I've had the pleasure of having him in my bed every night he's not at work. There's a notable difference between the amount of sleep I get when he's here versus when he's not. As in, I *don't* sleep when he's not.

I must've dozed off last night waiting for him to get home because I don't even remember him climbing into bed with me. My brain knew he was there. He chases away my nightmares.

CHAPTER 13

Madden

Sitting in the hospital waiting room, counting the seconds until the nurse will call me back for my x-ray. My legs bounce and I notice that there's almost no pain in my right leg anymore. In fact, I've been walking without a crutch for at least a week. I have a small hitch in my gait, but it's hardly noticeable. If only I could say as much for my hand.

"Madden Brody," a nurse calls out. I jump up and Thane pats my back, wishing me 'good luck' before I head back, leaving him to wait for me.

The x-rays are quick and then I'm lead to the doctor's office to hear the results.

"Good news Mr. Brody, the fracture appears to be healed. So, you can resume all normal activity. How are you feeling overall?"

"Fine. My hand is the worst, still really shaky."

The doctor nods.

"That's to be expected and may not improve. Nerve damage isn't like muscle damage, you can't exercise your way out of it. In time it may begin to heal, new fibers may grow beneath the intact insulating tissue until it reaches a muscle or sensory receptor. However, that also means that in time it may *not* heal. At this point it's up to your body. Time will tell," he explains.

"I understand," I grumble. That is *not* what I wanted to hear.

I'm edgy as I make my way back out to Thane, my mind running over and over the fact that I've likely lost everything. I've lost my career and my identity. *Time will tell,* fuck that.

"How'd it go?" Thane asks when I reach him.

"Leg's fine, hand's fucked," I bite out, storming past him and out the front of building. Thane jogs to keep up.

"Madden, hold up. What did he say?"

I stop in front of his car with my arms crossed over my chest until he unlocks it and I climb in with a huff like a petulant child. Once Thane starts driving I answer his question.

"He said the nerve damage may or may not heal and there's nothing I can do either way. I may never be able to tattoo again, or create any art for that matter. I have fucking nothing," I seethe. Thane flinches like I've slapped him, but I'm too pissed about the shitty hand I've been dealt to realize how hurtful my words were.

In order to avoid further conversation, I crank the radio up and look out the window.

When we get home I'm still in a rage, slamming my car door and stomping toward my bedroom with a storm of emotions in my chest. I want to scream and cry and fucking punch something.

When I get to my bedroom and attempt to slam my door, Thane catches it but stays on the outside of the room.

"I know you're upset, but why don't you try to calm down and we'll talk this through. It's not as bad as it seems." Thane's calm tone makes me want to rip my hair out.

"It's not alright. Nothing is alright!" I spin and grab a glass of water off my bedside table and whip it against the nearest wall, reveling in the loud shattering sound.

Thane regards me with caution, a war seeming to go on behind his eyes.

"Madden, you need to see a therapist. This is getting completely out of hand. You're one step away from being an agoraphobe, you're not dealing with all of the emotions caused by the healing process and the trauma you went through." Thane presses, a mixture of panic and embarrassment mingle in my gut.

"I'm sorry I'm not some badass marine like your boyfriend Zade," I snap, my entire body vibrating with the need to lash out, turn the spotlight off my problems and find a way to make all of this someone else's fault.

"You can't be jealous of Zade. *You* are my boyfriend, he's a friend I used to fool around with because it was convenient for both of us. Which is completely beside the point. You need to get help,

Madden. I'm worried about you."

"Why don't you fuck off," I suggest with a bitter bite to my words before giving him the finger and slamming the door to my bedroom with Thane on the outside.

I half expect him to chase after me, to press the issue. Part of me wants him to. He's right, I'm fucked up. It's fucking humiliating that Thane can face so much and be fine. He was in that club with me. He heard the screams and experienced the horror emanating through the crowd as people pressed for the exit. He's fine, though. He's sleeping like a baby, back at work saving lives. He's moved forward. And I fucking can't.

I crawl into bed and bury my face in my pillow, letting out an inhuman scream of frustration and self-hatred. Why am I so fucked up? Why can't I even leave the fucking house without having a panic attack? Why can't I sleep?

The sound of the front door shutting reverberates through the hallway. A whimper escapes my throat, fear settles in the pit of my stomach, and I hate myself for being so weak. I'm a grown man, I shouldn't need someone to come over and babysit me.

I just want the pain to go away.

This thought hits me with the force of a freight train and drains all the energy from my body. I sag down onto my bed with a broken sob. I'm afraid to close my eyes for fear of the nightmares I might have. But I'm equally afraid to keep them open because being awake and alone is agony.

My hands are trembling as I push myself to my feet. I need the pain to stop, and there's only one thing I know that can do that.

I'm alone, but for some reason I feel the need to sneak up the stairs to Thane's room, feeling a guilty thrill. Every cell in my body is at odds, shouting at me to stop, I kicked the drug habit once and I don't know if I can do it a second time. Another part of me is vibrating with anticipation of a long resisted high.

I push open Thane's door and peek inside. It's weird, but I haven't come up to his bedroom before. We've made a habit of sleeping in my room since for the first few months I was here I couldn't manage the stairs. Thane's bedroom is tidy yet welcoming, and his bed looks warm and inviting. I can imagine that the sheets must be bathed in his delicious musk.

If I were Thane, where would I stash my boy-friend's drugs?

Hot shame prickles at my skin as I glance over and see the bottle of Oxy sitting on the top of his dresser. He didn't hide them, because he trusted that I wasn't going to take them. I want to be the person he thinks I am. I want to be strong and able to cope with everything. I want to be worthy of all the amazing love Thane has to give. But none of that wanting is enough to stop me from reaching out and grasping the bottle like it's mana from heaven.

It takes me three tries to get the bottle open thanks to my shaking hands. As soon as several little white pills tumble into my hand I breathe a sigh of relief. The part of me that's strong enough to resist is relegated to a quiet corner of my brain, unable to stop what the rest of me needs so badly.

I throw back three pills and swallow them dry.

As soon as I've taken the pills a sob tears from deep in my chest. *What have I done?* Thane trusted me. Adam trusted me. A sinister voice in the back of my mind whispers that it might be better to take them all. It would end the pain for good. I wouldn't have to face the disappointment in Thane or Adam's eyes when they find out I've relapsed. I could finally sleep.

Before I know it, I've swallowed a whole handful of Oxy as the tears flow freely down my face. I don't want to feel any of this anymore.

I toss the empty bottle on the floor and crawl into Thane's bed, pulling his blankets up around me, pretending it's his strong arms holding me. Another broken sob escapes my lips as I imagine Thane coming home to find me.

That thought makes me cold all the way to my bones. I can't do that to him. He saved my life. He's done everything possible to care for me. It will kill him to find me that way. *What have I done?*

I fumble for my cell phone in my pocket, the edges of the world already growing fuzzy as the

Oxy starts to kick in. After several tries, I manage to dial the call.

"Nine-one-one, what is your emergency?" A pleasant female voice asks.

"I don't want to die," I manage to whisper into the phone before the world goes black.

Thane

I'm edgy and distracted as I enter the firehouse. I wish I knew how to convince Madden to get help. I need to find a way to convince him that needing help coping with everything doesn't make him weak.

I'm not even settled in when the alarm sounds. *It's going to be one of those fucking nights*.

I hustle to get my gear on, the other men doing the same, and then hop onto the truck.

As the fire engine pulls out of the station, I hear the driver ask the address and ice fills my veins when the response from the dispatcher is too familiar.

"That's my house," I mutter, feeling like I've gone numb.

Hayden's eyes widen as he absorbs my words.

"It's going to be alright," he says, placing a reassuring hand over mine. When we pull up, there aren't any signs of a fire. That's not uncommon, especially if the emergency operator doesn't have any indication of the problem, they just send everyone. I climb out of the truck and make to sprint for the door, but strong arms come around my shoulders to restrain me. "You'd better wait here, just in case."

"No," I argue, struggling against the hold as several of other men enter my house with caution. *It was an accidental call. The address was wrong. I fell asleep and am having a nightmare.* My heart thunders in my ears as I wait for someone to re-emerge and give me a goddamn clue about what's happening.

When an ambulance pulls up one of my men appears again in the front door and waves the paramedics over. *Fuck, no, no, this isn't happening..*

"Hayden, you have to let me go. I need to know..."

"No, you don't. Let the other guys do their job. You'll only be in the way. Everything will be fine."

"You don't know that," I argue in a weak voice.

Moments later they're all coming out of the house with a prone form on the stretcher.

He's not moving.

My knees give out at the sight. Between the marines and my career as a firefighter I've seen a lot of disturbing things. I've been in a lot of bad situations. Never in my life have I felt so much terror deep in my bones. I can't breathe.

Hayden's grip on me weakens a fraction and I take the opportunity to buck him. Stumbling my way over to the paramedics as they load him onto the ambulance, my tongue feels too big in my mouth, my hands are shaking violently.

"What happened? Tell me he's okay."

I climb into the ambulance without waiting to be told I'm allowed. One paramedic attaches oxygen and then begins to hook Madden up to a variety of machines. When a subtle beeping sound starts the tightness in my chest eases a fraction. He's alive.

"It looks like an overdose." He hands me an empty pill bottle and I stare at it, trying to force my brain to put the pieces together.

"This was a full bottle. He took them all?"

"It appears so."

"Is he going to be okay?" I reach for Madden's lifeless hand and squeeze it, hoping on some level he knows I'm there.

"We got to him pretty fast. We're going to need to induce vomiting, give him activated charcoal to absorb the toxins, and probably be at the hospital for 72 hour psych hold. Looks like a suicide attempt."

"What?" That's can't be true. I know Madden was struggling to cope, but it couldn't have been so bad he'd kill himself.

"Sorry. Is he your husband?"

I nod, knowing I'll have more access at the hospital if I lie. I manage to find enough wherewithal to pull out my phone and text Hayden to tell him to let the captain know what happened so they're not expecting me back to finish my shift.

Then I send a short text to Adam- because I know he'll want to know what's happening with Madden- saying simply 'Madden. Hospital'. He'll figure it out.

Madden

"Just tell me what the fuck happened," Adam's pissed off voice permeates my unconscious state.

"No. If Madden wants to tell you when he wakes up then he will," I hear Thane argue.

My eyelids are too heavy to open, which is okay because I don't think I'm ready to face Adam's ire. Lying still so they don't know I'm starting to wake, I strain my memory to figure out what I'm doing in a hospital again. Even with my eyes closed the smell and quiet beep-beep-beep is a dead giveaway.

Adam huffs in frustration and it sounds like he plops down in a chair beside my bed. I hate that I've upset him, after everything he's done for me. *Everything he's done for me.* That shakes the memory loose. I took Oxy. I took *way* too much Oxy.

I groan at my own stupidity and the air in the room stills. I dare to peek an eye open and find both Thane and Adam leaning over my bed, eyes laced with concern.

"Hey baby, how're you feeling?" Thane asks, giving my hand a gentle squeeze. There are tense lines around his eyes and his shoulders are tense. He knows what happened. He knows I'm a useless junkie with a death wish.

"Fucking peachy," I mutter.

"Adam, can I have a few minutes with Madden?"

Adam frowns but leaves without comment. As soon as we're alone Thane drops into the chair beside my bed and leans his head forward, grasping my hand between his own and bringing his to his forehead. I can feel the tension and agony rolling off him in waves.

"Why?" Is the only word he manages to choke out.

As soon as I hear the broken cadence of his voice the dam breaks and tears begin to stream down my face.

"It wasn't on purpose. Not entirely, anyway. I was just so tired. I wanted a few minutes of peace from the torment in my brain. As soon as I took a few I was so ashamed. I knew you'd hate me. You're a marine and a firefighter, you're incredible. You deserve so much more than a fucking junkie loser."

My body is wracked with sobs, and in a flash I'm encased in Thane's arms.

"You should've come to me. I didn't know it was that bad. Please don't leave me like that. God, Madden, I love you so fucking much. Don't ever do that again." The front of my hospital gown grows damp with Thane's own tears as he buries his face in my chest and clings to me like I'm a life raft.

"Never, I promise. I'm so sorry. I'm so fucking sorry. I love you so much."

His mouth finds mine as our tears mix on our lips, me reveling in the feeling of being alive, and Thane- no doubt- reassuring himself I am.

The sound of the door opening forces us apart. I turn to find Doctor Grant, the same doctor who treated me eight weeks ago when I was brought in more than half dead. Instead of a caring expression like he wore before, he looks stern.

"I'm happy to say that we were able to rid your system of the pills soon enough that there was no permanent damage." I breathe a sigh of relief and nod at him to continue. "We're going to place you on a psyche hold and have you evaluated by a psychiatrist."

I tense at his words and shake my head 'no' rapidly.

"Baby, what's the problem?" Thane asks, giving my hand a reassuring squeeze.

"I can't," I whisper, tightness in my throat preventing me from speaking at a normal volume. "I *can't.*"

"It's not optional Mr. Brody. I can't release you until I'm sure there won't be another suicide attempt."

"Madden, it's not a bad idea to talk to someone," Thane says, his tone cautious. I know he's remembering this is exactly what we fought about before he left.

"I'm afraid." I admit.

"Why? The psychiatrist only wants to help."

I turn so I'm only facing Thane, I won't be able to say this if I think about Dr. Grant scrutinizing me.

"Remember when I told you that my parents wanted to send me to conversion therapy?" Thane nods in response so I continue. "Before that-before they knew for sure I was gay- they suspected. Starting when I was ten, they made me go to a therapist every week. I hated it. It was three hours of torture every week, where I had to sit in a room and a man would tell me how wrong and disgusting it was to have sexual feelings for another man. He'd say that if I thought about boys even for a second, I was a pervert and I was going to hell. They made me take pills that they said would help me, they just made me numb and tired."

"That's so fucked up," Thane says, his eyes flaming with outrage on my behalf. "What if I stay with you while you talk with the psychiatrist, would that help?"

"Would you? Can he?" I turn to ask the doctor. Dr. Grant nods his consent and I relax against my pillow. "Okay."

CHAPTER 14

Thane

Madden shifts and fidgets in the hospital bed, checking the time over and over with a deepening frown.

"Babe," I take his hand and kiss his knuckles. The gesture seems to soothe him a little. "Do you trust me to protect you?"

"Of course." The vehemence of his response warms me.

"Okay, then relax. The psychiatrist is just going to come in and chat with you. I'll be here the whole time. Nothing, and I mean *nothing* is going to harm you as long as I'm here. Understand?"

"Yes." Madden says and relaxes against his pillow.

A few minutes later when a middle-aged woman in a white coat walks in holding a clipboard, Madden tenses again.

"Hello, you must be Mr. Brody?" She smiles warmly and offers a hand to Madden.

"Yes. Call me Madden, please. And this is my boyfriend, Thane." He introduces me with an air of challenge, like he wants to gage the doctor's reaction to his sexual orientation.

"So nice to meet you, Thane." The doctor offers me her hand as well. *So far, so good.*

"He's going to stay, if that's okay?" Madden asks.

"Sure, whatever makes you most comfortable. Do you mind if I sit?"

Madden nods and the doctor sinks into a chair next to the bed. I settle onto the bed next to Madden and link our fingers to lend him some courage.

"Now, can you tell me a little bit about what led you here today?"

Madden hesitates for a moment but then launches into the tale of the nightclub shooting, his journey of physical healing, not being able to sleep, panic attacks when he tried to leave the house. His words cut me deep. I knew he was struggling, but I was blind to how much. I promised I'd take care of him and I failed.

It's not until his fingers wiggle against mine that I realize I've been crushing his hand in my grip. I ease up and take a deep breath, giving him a reassuring smile.

"From what you're telling me, Madden, it sounds like you have PTSD."

"That's pretty serious, right?" Madden asks in a small voice.

"It is, but it's also very manageable with the proper help. I'm going to recommend you seek therapy upon release, and I can give you a name of several colleagues who specialize in PTSD treatment."

"I don't want medication," Madden inter-jects.

"Okay, I'll be sure to only include names of psychologists who focus on cognitive behavior therapy. Before I can recommend your discharge, I need to know that you won't attempt suicide again."

Madden shakes his head violently.

"No, absolutely not. It was a mistake and an overreaction. I can promise you it will never happen again."

"And now that I understand the depth of what's going on, I can assure you I'll take better care of him," I pipe in.

She smiles at both of us and makes a few notes on the clipboard before telling Madden that he'll still have to remain for the rest of the 72-hour psyche hold, but after that he'll be free to go. She also promises to have the list of referrals in the discharge paperwork.

"That wasn't so bad, right?"

"No, not too bad," Madden agrees, resting his head on my shoulder. "I meant it, I promise I'm going to take this seriously. I'm going to get better."

"I know, and I'm going to be there for you every step of the way.

Madden

I never realized how boring a psyche hold

would be. I feel like a prisoner or a child, being checked on every hour and more or less confined to the hospital bed so they can keep track of me. I'm relieved when Adam shows up, but the concern in his eyes immediately has me feeling like shit.

Without saying a word Adam takes the chair that Thane had been occupying for the last thirty-six hours, before I forced him to go home and take a shower and have a nap.

"You going to tell me what happened?" Adam asks, looking at the television on the wall instead of at me. Hot shame washes over me. The condition of my employment was to never touch drugs again. I don't know if I'll ever be able to tattoo again or not, but what will I do if Adam flat out fires me? What if he tells me he can't even be friends with someone as weak as I am?

"You're going to hate me," I hedge in a whisper.

"I doubt that."

"I took the whole bottle of Oxy. I didn't mean to. Well, I did, but it wasn't planned. I was weak, so I took a few. Then, I felt so fucking ashamed and tired of trying to cope after...everything. So, I took more. I took enough to make the pain go away forever. I chickened out as soon as I took them and called 911." Hot tears of shame burn behind my eyes as I explain what happened.

Adam's quiet for a long time and I'm convinced he's trying to find a way to tell me I'm fired.

When he finally speaks his voice is rough like he's holding back tears.

"Why didn't you tell anyone it was that bad? Don't you know that we're all here for you? You should've called me, or Royal, or Gage. Fuck I'm sure Nash or Dani would've dropped everything to come over and sit with you, talk to you, make sure you were okay."

I swallow around the lump in my throat and nod.

"Am I fired?"

"What? No, of course not."

"But you said if I ever touched drugs again, I was out." I'm not sure why I'm arguing, if he isn't firing me, I should be over the moon.

"I said that when you were standing in my shop all twitchy and strung out. You've been clean for four years and you've gone through a major trauma. Don't get me wrong, if you make a habit out of relapsing, you're out. But I think I can overlook one slip-up."

"Thank you."

"Don't mention it. Madden, you can't do this again. I don't mean the drugs, I..." Adam's voice breaks and when I look over, I notice his eyes are shining with tears. "I can't lose you like I lost John. Promise me next time you feel that way you'll call me right away."

I nod my head rapidly, ready to agree to anything to keep Adam from crying. I never thought I'd see a gruff guy like Adam break down like this.

"I promise. I won't ever do anything like that again. I didn't want to die, not really," I explain. "As soon as I did it, I realized it was a mistake and called an ambulance."

A small sob escapes Adam's throat as he stands from the chair and pulls me into a fierce hug.

"I love you man, you're like my little brother. I can't lose two little brothers."

"I know." I pat his back as he hugs me and let a tear or two of my own escape.

"Alright, enough of this sappy bullshit," Adam says pulling away and wiping his eyes with a chuckle. "This television get any good channels?"

"Home sweet home," Thane says, echoing his words the first time he brought me here, after my last hospital stay. Maybe I should consider not making a habit of this.

"I'm glad to be out of the hospital. I felt like I was there forever," I complain as we step into the house. As soon as the door is closed behind us Thane's hands are around me, lifting me up and pulling me close. I wrap my legs around his waist and my arms around his neck and give in to the ferocity of his lips on mine.

"God, I need you. Is this okay?" Thane asks.

I nod and bury my fingers in his hair, yanking it to force him to kiss me again. His tongue dances with mine, his fingers holding me up by the thighs with a bruising force. All I want is more. More tongue, more skin, more Thane.

We must be on the same wavelength because we're in my bedroom before I even realize we were moving. Thane drops me onto my bed and looms over me with a hunger in his eyes I've never seen before.

"I need to be inside you," he says as he tugs my shirt over my head and his hands begin to slowly explore my chest and abdomen. It's not like he hasn't touched every inch of me before, but the reverence in his gaze is like this is the first time. I shiver at his intensity and nod my head in agreement. Yes, I want him to take me. I want him to remind me what it feels like to be alive.

In spite of the fervor of the kisses from only moments ago, now that he has me in bed agreeing to be his, he slows his pace to a crawl.

Thane's lips set to work memorizing every inch of my upper body, just as his hands had. He takes languid detours to all my favorite spots, like the sensitive area just behind my ear that loves to be nibbled, and more bruising bites along my collar bone. I squirm and buck and plead, but Thane refuses to be rushed.

When I reach between us to get my pants off, Thane grabs my hands and pins them over my head with a warning glare.

"Please," I beg, panting at the perfect feeling of being pinned beneath this man.

"Patience."

As his mouth journeys lower my entire body pulses in anticipation. Thane tongues every dip and curve of my abs, paying special attention to my scar from the shooting, and my latest tattoo. When he reaches my happy trail, he runs his nose through the coarse hairs and hums with satisfaction, sending a jolt of lust through my already desperate cock. He unbuttons my pants and lowers them, along with my boxer briefs, exposing my throbbing erection to the air. *Finally.* I whimper and thrust towards his face, but he gives me a wicked smile and continues his torturous exploration along my hips and down my thighs.

A pearly bead of pre-cum leaks from my tip, my balls tight and aching.

"Please," I beg again, and still it doesn't inspire Thane to hurry his pace.

He kneels at the foot of the bed and spreads my thighs further. He then takes each of my legs and hooks them over his shoulders. *Please, please, please, please.*

The first contact of his hot, smooth tongue against my puckered hole has me arching off the bed with a strangled curse.

Thane grasps my hips to hold me in place as he eats my ass like it's his last meal, alternating between long strokes and teasing flicks until I'm so close to coming I'm nearly in tears.

"I can't...Thane...Fucking *please.*" I cry and squirm, ready to promise him anything in the world if he'll just let me come already.

Thane pulls back and I gasp at the sudden loss. He doesn't leave me hanging for more than a few seconds before he's back with a condom on his dick and lube in his hand.

He returns to his place between my legs, at the foot of the bed only standing this time. He maneuvers me like I'm nothing more than a ragdoll, until I'm positioned with my legs straight up against his upper body, giving him all the access he needs.

I gasp in relief when his broad head presses against my entrance. *Yes, yes, fuck yes.*

Thane takes care to ease in gently, when all I want him to do is pound me into the bed until I can't remember my own name. As every cell in my body comes alive like an electric wire, I close my eyes and bask in every sensation. *This* is being alive. His thick cock filling me, his thrusts long and deep.

"Look at me," Thane commands, and my eyes pop open.

The look in his eyes guts me. Every ounce of love and fear and relief that he has inside of him are shining out clear as day through his eyes. I notice a single tear on his cheek and I reach up to wipe it away.

Thane lets my legs fall, his pace never faltering, as he pulls my mouth to his. The kiss isn't anything like I expected it to be. It's still filled with hunger, but it feels different. There is sorrow and promises there, too.

As we kiss, his thrusts become more frantic and I meet every one, needing him harder, deeper. I angle my hips so each stroke glides over my prostate.

"Oh god, Thane...I...fuck!"

My head falls back as I let every wave of ecstasy crash over me. I vaguely register Thane's own shout of pleasure and the feeling of his cock pulsing deep inside me. *Maybe I did die and go to heaven after all.*

Thane collapses on the bed beside me, both of us sweaty and panting for breath.

"I love you," Thane murmurs against my jaw before kissing my scruff and then shuffling us up the bed to get comfortable.

"We should get cleaned up," I suggest half-heartedly.

"Too tired, shower in the morning," Thane grunts before removing the condom and tossing it in the garbage can near my nightstand.

I yawn and let him pull me against his chest.

"I love you, too," I whisper to him in the dark before drifting off into a dreamless sleep.

"Are you sure you're going to be okay having Royal take you to meet with your new therapist?" Thane asks, worrying his bottom lip.

"You have work, so yes I'll be fine," I assure

him for the hundredth time. Thane pulls me close kissing my jaw and then my lips.

"Call or text me if you need to."

"I will," I kiss him one last time before shooing him out the door. He's already missed out on work because of me, I'm not about to let him be late today too.

I tidy up around the house while I wait for Royal, noting how perfectly domestic it feels to be cleaning up after Thane.

Sitting in the waiting room of my new therapist's office, I shift and fidget in my seat. The receptionist seemed friendly when I came in, but who knows what this doctor will be like. Royal had offered to stay with me, but I told him I didn't need babysitting and that he could come pick me up in an hour.

"Dr. Marvin is ready for you, Mr. Brody," The receptionist informs me.

I rise from the chair, my knees trembling so badly I almost collapse right back into it. *This will be fine. I'm an adult now, if the doctor says anything derogatory or offensive I can walk right out.* Thane had repeatedly reminded me of that fact last night and this morning, adding that if that happens I'd better let him know so he can come down here and give Doctor Marvin a piece of his mind.

I manage to make it across the small reception area and to the doctor's office without my legs giving out. The door opens and I'm surprised to find myself face to face with a man who looks to be in his early thirties, with kind eyes, and a friendly smile.

"You must be Madden, come on in." He steps back and gestures into his office.

"It's nice to meet you Dr. Marvin."

"Please, call me Eric. I've always been uncomfortable with formalities."

I nod and take a deep breath. He seems nice so far, maybe this won't be so bad. There's a couch pushed against the far wall, a desk, a comfortable looking chair, and a coffee table. Eric takes the comfortable chair and picks up a notebook and pen from the coffee table before gesturing toward the couch. I sink down and let my eyes wander for a moment, taking in the office. It's more welcoming than I was expecting, with paintings on the walls and a few plants near the window. My eyes land on a photo on the desk of Eric and another man with a young girl between them. They're all smiling at the camera like they're the happiest people alive.

"That's a nice picture," I say. Eric turns to see which one I'm looking at and his eyes brighten.

"That's my husband and our daughter."

The last bit of tension eases out of my shoulders at the word 'husband'.

"You have a beautiful family."

"Thank you. Now, why don't we talk about

what brings you in to see me today."

"Didn't the doctor from the hospital send you my file?" I ask. I'm pretty sure that's how referrals usually work.

"She did," he confirms. "But I'd rather hear from you. We can start anywhere you like. If you want to talk about what lead you to the hospital a few days ago, that's fine. If you prefer to start further back, that's okay, too. This is about you, I'm just here to help you to work through it. Okay?"

"Okay," I swallow and take a deep breath before launching into where this all started. My parents, being homeless, my addiction, Adam saving me, my failed relationships, the night I was shot, and finally Thane. I didn't know I could tell someone so much in under an hour. But the words just kept spewing from me, out of my control.

As I talked, one thing started to nag at the back of my mind. And the more I prattled on about Thane the more obvious it became to me.

"Do you think I'm too dependent on Thane?" I blurt out.

"Do *you* think you are?" *Ugh, psychologist speak.*

"I didn't, but now that I'm thinking about it...yeah, kind of. I can't sleep without him, he calms my panic attacks, he's taken care of me since the shooting. I love him for that, but I want to be able to take care of myself. I don't want our whole relationship to be about Thane rescuing me, especially not from myself."

"I think that's very astute," Eric says, making a few notes in his notebook. "It looks like our time is up, but we can explore that more in our next session on Thursday, okay?"

I mutter something in the affirmative, my whole body going numb as I realize what my revelation means.

As I leave Eric's office I realize that it's not just Thane I've been too dependent on. I've been leaning on Adam to take care of me for years. I'm not a child, I'm an adult and I need to start acting like one.

"You okay?" Royal asks as I climb into his car. "Did therapy go alright?"

"I'm fine," I assure him. "The doctor was nice. He's gay, so that was a relief."

"That's good. This is going to help a lot," Royal puts a reassuring hand on my shoulder and gives it a squeeze, before putting the car in reverse and pulling out of the parking space.

"Can we stop over at my apartment and get my car?"

Royal glances at me out of the corner of his eye with apprehension.

"Are you okay to drive?"

"My leg is healed; my hand still kind of sucks but my car isn't manual."

"No, I meant…"

My blood pulses hot with a mixture of shame and anger.

"You think I'm going to drive my car off a

bridge or something? There are a lot easier ways to kill myself," I snap.

"Okay, fine, we'll go get your car," Royal gripes, still throwing suspicious glances my way.

"It's time I stopped depending on other people to take care of me, that's all."

"We're your friends, we don't mind."

"I don't care if you mind. *I* mind. I'm an adult." Even as I'm bitching at Royal I know I'm being an asshole. All he's done is chauffer me around and babysit me. It's not his fault. It's my fault. I'm the one who's weak. I'm the one who's pathetic.

Royal doesn't say another word as he drives me to Adam's apartment. Well, technically my apartment but I don't see moving back in there. Letting Adam coddle me is no better than being too dependent on Thane.

"Thanks," I mutter as I hop out of Royal's car near the parking garage and go in search of my car.

The entire drive back to Thane's my mind is busy making a plan. I hate the plan, but I also need it. The thought of leaving Thane is like a punch in the gut. How will I ever heal and become strong if I let him prop me up now, though? How will I ever be a man who deserves Thane? I have to hurt him now so we can have a chance at a future later.

Thane

"Honey, I'm home," I call out as I step into the house after my twenty-four hour shift. An anxious feeling instantly washes over me. The house is too quiet, too still. I know without even looking that Madden isn't here, but I check anyway. When I find every room empty and tidy I force myself to take a deep breath and not panic. Madden could be anywhere. He could be with Royal, or Adam, or hell he might even have gone for a short walk and will be back any second. Something feels off. Don't ask me how I know, I just do.

I walk into the kitchen to grab a glass of water and find a note on the counter.

Thane,
I hate myself for doing this to you. I also hate clichés, but this one happens to be 100% true: it's not you, it's me. You are amazing. You are everything I've ever wanted in a life partner. The thing is, I need some time to work on me. I know your first instinct is going to be to come storming after me to make sure I'm safe and taken care of. I promise I'm not going to hurt myself. I just need to learn to stand on my own two feet. I am so sorry. I hope one day you can understand and forgive me.

Love,
Madden

I re-read the note at least four times, unable to believe this is really happening. My stomach feels like it's dropped out and my hands are shaking as it sinks in. Madden left me? He left without even telling me or giving me a chance to talk things through.

Needing an outlet for the tumultuous emotions coursing through me, I spin and sink my fist into the nearest wall, reveling in the pain that shoots up my arm and the satisfying crunch of the plaster.

The sound of my phone vibrating pulls me back to reality. I scramble to grab it, praying it's Madden. Without even looking at the display I answer and bring it to my ear.

"Madden?" *please, please be Madden.*

The silence on the other end goes on a few beats too long before the person on the other end responds.

"Fuck, Royal's going to flip."

"Zade?"

"Yeah, Royal wanted me to call and make sure Madden seemed okay. I take it he's not there?"

"No." I can barely force the words past my lips as the energy seems to drain out of my body and I sink down onto the kitchen floor. "He left me. There's a note. I don't know where..."

"Alright, I'm coming over there and we're going to deal with this the only logical way, by getting totally shitfaced."

"What about Madden? What if he's not okay?" I protest.

"He's an adult, he's capable of taking care of himself. I'll let Royal know and his friends can deal with that. You're *my* friend and I'm going to come over and do my friendship duties."

"Okay," I agree, unable to argue anymore.

When I hang up the phone I can't resist dialing Madden's number. I know he said he needed space, but what the fuck? With each ring I feel my temper rising. Who the fuck bails with nothing more than a note? By the time his voicemail picks up I'm fuming.

"What the fuck, Madden? I can't believe you left with nothing more than a goddam 'dear John' letter. I thought I fucking meant something to you," I rage into the phone. "Did you stop for one second to consider how this would make me feel? Or were you too busy worrying about yourself? You know what, fuck you." When I smash my thumb against the 'end' button I reflect on how much more satisfying it would've been to slam the phone down to hang up. My muscles twitch with the urge to hurl my phone against the fucking wall.

The cavalry arrives in the form of Zade with a bottle of whiskey less than ten minutes later. He takes one look at the hole in the wall and nods in understanding.

I'm still on the kitchen floor so Zade sinks down beside me, uncaps the bottle of whiskey and passes it to me. I take a healthy gulp and enjoy the burn.

An hour and approximately one metric shit-ton of whiskey later, Zade has convinced me to move from the kitchen floor to the couch. I'm splayed out, trying not to think about the night Madden and I fooled around on this vary spot. The night we sort of made things official.

I take another gulp of whiskey, desperate to forget.

"Hey, you want to fuck?" I ask Zade. Fucking Zade would be a great way to forget my humiliation and feel like I'm getting back at Madden for being an asshole.

"Pass," Zade says, taking the whiskey from me and taking a drink.

"What the hell? Why not?" I whine. I'd be embarrassed for sounding so childish if I weren't so drunk.

"For starters, because you'd regret it when you sober up and that would be a dumb fucking reason to ruin our friendship. And secondly, when I first met Royal he threatened my life if I ever came between you and Madden. I'm ninety-five percent sure I could take him, but he's a little crazy so I'd rather not risk it."

"God you're so whipped now. I never thought I'd see you like this."

"Like you can talk," Zade teases.

"You think I should give him space or go find him?"

"I'd give him space. You can't force him. He'll come around. And, until then, we drink."

"Good plan." I take another gulp from the bottle. "Do you think I have a hero complex?"

"You're a former marine and a firefighter, it's a pretty safe bet to say you've got a hero complex."

"I think that's why Madden thinks I liked him," I confide. "Like I didn't like him for him, I liked to save him or some shit."

"Is it?"

"Of course not!" I slam the whiskey bottle down and glare at Zade. "He brought color to my life. I didn't even realize it before I met him, but I wasn't really living. I went to work and I came home, that was it. It was miserable. I didn't have any friends because I didn't know who I could trust to tell about my sexuality. Actually, no, that's a lie. I didn't *want* to let anyone close. I thought I was content being in my own bubble. I had no idea what I was missing until I met him."

"So tell him that. Let him know that he's not just a victim for you to save," Zade suggests.

"Maybe I should give him the time he asked for," I quietly resolve, flinching in shame at the voicemail I left him just a few hours ago. "The minute I laid eyes on him, and he was flirting and laughing with the bartender, I was drawn to him. He was so vibrant and full of life. But the shooting robbed him of that. I just want to see that again. If giving him time will bring that man back, then I'll give him all the time he needs."

Madden

I erase Thane's voicemail without listening to it. I know it'll either be him telling me I'm a dickhead or begging me to come home. I can't take hearing either.

After the fifth consecutive call from Royal I decide I'd better answer before he sends the National Guard out looking for me.

"I'm fine, relax."

"*Relax*? You've got to be fucking kidding me," Royal mutters seemingly to himself. "I asked you if there was something wrong after your therapy appointment. I fucking *knew* I shouldn't have dropped you off to get your car. Where are you? I'm coming to get you and bringing you home where you belong."

"Royal, stop for a second and let me explain." I flop down on the stiff sheets of the motel bed, my phone still pressed to my ear. "First of all, I'm okay. I'm not planning to hurt myself, I'm not on drugs, I'm safe. I need some time, that's all."

"Time? Time for what?"

"Time to stand on my own two feet. I've relied on other people to carry me for too long."

"There's no shame in letting someone help you up when you fall," Royal argues in a gentle tone.

"No, there's not," I agree, "But, there is shame in letting someone carry you around when your own two legs work fine."

"Is there any talking you out of this?"

"No. I'll call you in a few days. I want to sort

myself out a little and then you can come see for yourself that I'm not Sylvia Plath-ing it. Okay?"

"I guess so," Royal grumbles.

"Thanks, man."

"Thane's freaking out, you know," Royal adds.

"I left him a note. You can tell him you talked to me and I'm fine. I wasn't trying to hurt him. I hope he'll forgive me eventually."

"I can't speak to that, but I guess I'll let you go. You call if you need *anything*, understand?"

"I promise," I assure him before we both say goodbye and hang up the phone.

CHAPTER 15

Madden

"How have you been doing the past few days?" Eric asks as I settle onto the couch in his office.

"Eh, I'm alright," I shrug.

"Do tell," Eric prompts, pen poised near his notebook.

"I'm doing my hand exercises, but the damn shaking. I can't…" I'm surprised how quickly I can get emotional about this subject. I want to shut the conversation down and talk about something else. It's too much. This is why I'm here, right? I need to face this stuff so I don't freak out and try to off myself again. "I don't know who I am without my art."

"You're more than your art. Tell me who is Madden Brody?"

I let out a humorless laugh, studying my hands like the secret of life is written on them.

"Madden Brody is a homeless junkie. Madden Brody is a nobody."

"I'm sure that's not true Madden. I'm going to give you homework this week. I want you to make a list of ten things that are uniquely Madden

Brody. Ten *positive* things. And I want you to practice affirmations. It's going to feel silly at first, but I think you'll find that the more you do them the better you'll feel."

"What are affirmations?" I ask warily.

"You stand in front of the mirror, look yourself in the eyes, and say 'I am important. The world is a better place because I'm here'. Okay?"

"I guess." It does sound stupid, but it can't hurt to try it. "And *this* is supposed to cure my PTSD?"

"We're not here to cure your PTSD. We're here to identify your triggers and learn to manage them, as well as learning techniques to manage the panic attacks."

My heart sinks. *I'll never be cured.* That's all I can hear him telling me, repeating on a loop in my mind. I'll never be normal again.

"I moved out of Thane's place," I blurt. "Right after our session the other day I packed up my stuff and left. I'm staying at a hotel for the moment while I look for a place."

"What happened? Did the two of you have a fight?"

"No, nothing like that. I was kind of a dick actually, I just left without giving him the courtesy of saying goodbye. I left a note."

"A note?"

"Ugh, god, I'm the worst," I groan, burying my face in my hands. "But I need to learn to stand on my own two feet. I've been relying on other people to take care of me my whole life. The last time no one took care of me I was a homeless junkie. I need to know that I can do this, on my own."

Eric regards me for several seconds before he nods.

"I hate to see you without a support system during such a difficult time. I understand your need to stand on your own feet. Don't be afraid to ask for help when you need it, okay?"

"Okay."

The rest of the therapy session goes by quickly, mainly focusing on my history with 'therapy' and how that likely has contributed to my PTSD.

I take several deep breaths, standing out-side the craft store. I'd considered buying paints and canvasses online, but I feel the need to at-tempt to face my fears. Eric explained to me that during a panic attack my brain believes I'm ac-tually in mortal danger. I might feel like I can't breathe or like I'm about to have a heart attack, but those things aren't real. I can ride it out and move past it, but it won't be comfortable or fun.

Clenching my hands into fists to curb the trembling, I step forward through the automatic sliding doors. My heart is hammering in my chest, but each step into the store that doesn't end in certain death seems to calm my nerves.

I scan the aisles in an effort to get what I came for and get out. *Acrylic paint, bingo!*

The array of colors before me has my mind dancing with possibilities. I haven't painted before, always tending towards drawing and tattooing for my artistic escapes. My hand is finally capable of fine motor movements again, but the tremor caused by the nerve damage hasn't improved. I'm hoping paint will be more forgiving than pencil or charcoal.

By the time I've chosen a dozen colors and a few small and medium canvases I realize that I can breathe, and my heartrate is almost normal.

I did it!

It takes extreme effort not to break out into a victory dance then and there. I'm sure I look like I've got a few screws loose when I purchase my paint supplies with a grin on my face like I've just won the lottery. Fuck it, I'm going to celebrate my personal accomplishment.

It takes me two more days to work up the balls to send a group text to Adam, Royal, Gage, Nash, and Dani and invite them to come visit me so they can see I'm doing well.

When they knock on the door of my hotel room around eight, I shuffle my painting stuff to the side so it's not taking up the middle of the small room, and then go to answer the door.

My friends spill in, filling the cramped space and all at once demanding to know how I am and what the fuck I was thinking disappearing like that.

"Don't bust my balls on this, please. I needed time. It wasn't anything personal."

"Tell that to Thane, he's a fucking mess," Royal accuses, his blue eyes hard and icy.

Guilt twists my gut.

"I didn't want to hurt him," I argue feebly.

"Well, you can want in one hand and shit in the other and see which fills up first."

"Alright, cool it Royal. Whatever's between Thane and Madden is between them," Adam says, his authoritative tone firmly closing the topic, for which I am grateful. "You're painting?"

"Uh, yeah," I gesture toward the paintings I'd been working on for the last two days. "They're more therapy than anything. I wasn't *making* anything, just getting the emotions out, you know?"

"That's art man," Adam laughs and steps towards my paintings to examine them. "These are awesome. You should put these in an art consignment shop, I bet people would buy them."

"Maybe," I rub the back of my neck, ignoring the twinge of annoyance at Adam trying to make my life choices for me again. His intentions are good, I know that.

"You sure you want to stay here? You can come back home, no one's going to think you're weak or anything," Gage presses.

"It's not about what you guys think. I need to do this for me. I have plenty of money in my account right now to figure out what I want to do. I need to come up with a plan in case I can't tattoo anymore and I need space to think things through."

"Alright," Adam agrees with a sigh before pulling me into a hug.

After they hang out for a little while they all decide it's time to call it a night and head out, each making me promise I'll call if I need anything and threatening to kick my ass if I don't come home soon. As soon as I'm alone the guilt created by Royal's earlier comment sits heavy on my chest.

I grab my phone and force myself to make the call.

"Madden?" Thane answers on the second ring sounding wary yet hopeful.

"Yeah," I respond, crawling into bed and pulling the covers over my head as I listen to Thane's breathing through the phone. "I'm sorry."

"I don't understand why." Thane sounds so broken my hands itch to touch him and hold him. Everything in me demands I beg forgiveness and plead with him to take me back.

"You are so amazing and so good at protecting me and taking care of me. I was relying on you too much. When I was talking to my therapist the other day it hit me that I went from letting Adam take care of me to letting you take care of me. The last time I took care of myself I was a homeless junkie. That's not a ringing endorsement for my adulting skills. I need to stand on my own two feet at least for a little while so that I know that I can."

Thane's quiet for several long seconds before he lets out a long sigh.

"I get that. Why didn't you talk to me instead? Why don't you come home and I promise I'll pull back on the protective instinct?"

"I want to, I really do. It's the same as my drug addiction, though. I don't think I could take a small dose without going overboard."

"So what you're saying is that my love is your drug?" Thane asks, I almost think he's serious until he starts singing the Ke$ha song in a high falsetto. I can almost picture him shaking his hips and raising his arms over his head as he sings and carries on. My heart clenches with longing even as I laugh at his antics.

"I love you, I hope you can forgive me for this."

"I probably shouldn't admit this because it gives you way too much power in this relationship, but I think I could forgive you for just about anything. Just promise me you're taking care of yourself?"

"I promise. I'd better go," I say before I can change my mind and tell Thane I'm coming home now. *Home.* That's its own question. Where is my home now? Back with Adam doesn't feel like it fits anymore. I want my home to be with Thane, but it feels like rushing the relationship. I guess that's an item for my agenda tomorrow- find a place to call home for a little while.

"Okay. Goodnight, babe. Please call me again so I'm not sitting here going out of my mind with worry?"

"I will. Night."

Hanging up the phone is one of the most difficult things I've ever done.

Thane

Letting Madden off the phone was one of the most difficult things I've ever done. I understand now why he felt the need to take a step back. Don't get me wrong, I'm still pissed that he up and left without the courtesy of telling me to my face, and we will definitely be discussing that issue before we reconcile in the future. Now isn't the time to rage and point fingers. Now is the time to let Madden know I'm here whenever he's ready to talk.

Madden

Get an apartment, *check.* It's nothing fancy, and it's pathetically small, but it's all mine. I stand in the middle of the living room and allow myself a mental high-five for my awesome adulting. Step two, figure out a new career path in the event tattooing is permanently out. I grudgingly accept that Adam had a good idea about the consignment shop. And, after I hung up with Thane last night, I stayed up until dawn painting two more pieces.

I'm going to have to go get more canvases today, too. While I'm at it, I also should stop at Rainbow House.

Pleased with myself for planning a whole day out of the house and being productive, I practice the affirmations that Eric told me to do.

"I am awesome. I'm totally killing it right now. Way to go, Madden, you are the man." I feel like a bit of a tool talking to myself like this.

Before I head out the door I grab a stress ball, or more accurately, stress balls, as it is shaped like testicles- that I purchased off Amazon, and shove it in my pocket. I've been reading up on techniques for managing panic attacks and one of the recommendations is to have something to play with to keep your brain calm. Another is to chew gum, because your brain is programmed to believe that if you're eating you can't be in mortal danger. So, armed with my balls and a pack of gum, I slip on my shoes and head out to face the world.

The consignment shop has a bit of a hipster vibe, not much of a surprise in Seattle. When I show the owner pictures on my phone of my paintings, he gladly offers me space in the shop to put them for sale and I agree to bring them by tomorrow. I manage the whole interaction with minimal anxiety, so I give myself another mental high-five.

At the hobby store while I shop for more paint supplies I get a shady look from a guy. When my heart starts to beat too quickly, I reach into my pocket and start kneading the squishy testicles that are meant to relieve stress, and counting my breaths.

By the time I have myself under control, I glance back in the direction of the man and find that he's gone. I let out a sigh of relief. Yes, I freaked out, but I also managed to get it under control all on my own. That's progress.

I'm still a little shaky as I straighten up, and the urge to call Thane, just to hear his soothing voice is nearly overwhelming. I continue counting my breaths to keep my brain distracted, grab the necessary supplies, and make my way to the front to pay.

The last stop is Rainbow House.

When I pull into the parking lot my stomach does a flip. Thane's car is parked in front of the building.

Thane

"Have you ever killed a man?" asks Derek, a fifteen-year-old boy who's been living at Rainbow House for over a year after his dad beat the shit out of him for coming out as transgender.

I open my mouth to answer when Madden walks in. My breath catches in my chest. It's been a week since I last saw him, but it feels like a fucking lifetime. Every cell in my body is screaming out for me to go over there, shove him against the nearest wall, and kiss the hell out of him. Instead, I settle for a wave and a tight smile. Madden nods and returns the smile before getting mobbed by some of the kids.

"Can we do art today?" One boy asks.

"As a matter of fact, we can. I brought paint stuff, but I'm going to need help bringing it in from my car. Who wants to help?"

A handful of kids volunteer with enthusiasm.

Over the next two hours while Madden teaches the kids some painting techniques, and then supervises as they all let loose on their canvases, I sit back and watch. I start to notice something about Madden. He's standing taller, laughing more freely, he's glowing. He reminds me of the man I first spotted in the club, flirting with the bartender. My heart swells. I hate that he left me the way he did, but it looks like he was right about what he needed to heal.

Every so often Madden catches my eye and offers me a small smile, which I return. As far as the kids are concerned, there's not much reason for me to still be here. I've been upstaged by what has largely devolved into finger painting. I can't tear my eyes away from Madden. I can't bring myself to leave while there's still the opportunity to soak up his presence for a few extra minutes.

"Hey Thane," Madden approaches me as the kids are cleaning up.

"Hey." I force myself to play it cool. He was right, this time is good for him. And if he needs it then I'm not going to force him to come back until he's ready.

"I don't want to send mixed signals or anything, but I was wondering if you'd like to see my new place? We could order a pizza and watch *Sons of Anarchy*, like old times."

"New place?"

"Yeah, I...uh...got an apartment. It's the first apartment I've ever rented on my own, I signed a lease and everything." The way his face lights up as he tells me such a mundane detail forces any hurt and anger I'd been harboring into remission.

"That sounds nice," I agree. "Don't you dare try to take advantage of me, though."

"Wouldn't dream of it," Madden assures me with false modesty.

Madden's place is small, but nice.

"Sorry it's so bare. I just moved in yesterday so I haven't had the chance to decorate or anything."

"Tell me what you're envisioning in terms of decorations." I prompt, standing in the middle of the room, looking around at all the potential of the space.

Madden brightens and launches into detailed description of his plans for the room.

When the pizza arrives, we sit on the floor with the pizza on the floor between us and his laptop set up in front of us.

"I should've thought about the fact that I don't have a couch before I invited you over."

"It's not a big deal. I'm glad you invited me to see it."

I notice that as we've been sitting together on the floor arguing over sex positions for our fantasy threesome with Charlie Hunnam we've unconsciously been drifting closer together. Now our thighs and shoulders are touching but neither of us say anything, nor do we move to put space between us. I have every intention of respecting his space and need for time, but I don't see how a little proximity could hurt anything.

When his head comes down on my shoulder I hold my breath for fear I'll do something to ruin this moment.

"Thank you for everything," he says, so quiet it's almost a whisper.

"What are you thanking me for, babe?" I ask, offering him my crust, which he gladly accepts.

"Giving me space to figure shit out. I miss you a lot."

"I miss you, too." I brush a kiss against the top of his head and take a deep breath, filling my lungs with his scent. "I should probably get going."

"Oh." His tone is resigned as he leans away.

"Hey," I turn his face toward me and look into his eyes. "I don't *want* to go, I'm trying to respect your need for space and if I stay any longer, I'm going to beg you to let me stay the night. That would be extremely embarrassing, wouldn't it?"

"Yes it would," Madden laughs and then without warning leans forward and presses his lips to mine in a chaste kiss. "Thanks for coming over. We should do this again soon. Maybe after I get a couch."

"A couch would be good," I agree.

CHAPTER 16

Madden

"How are you doing this week, Madden?" Eric asks.

"Better," I answer with a smile. "I feel like I'm taking care of myself for a change. My paintings are selling well at the consignment shop so I'm thinking of setting up an Etsy page or something. And I saw Thane this week. We hung out, it was nice."

"That's great. I'll admit, I was concerned when you cut yourself off from your support system so abruptly, but it's clear this is what you needed."

I nod, appreciating the validation.

"I feel stronger than I've ever felt before."

"I'm glad to hear that. I would still encourage you to consider joining a drug support group. If you're interested I run one, and it's free of all the religious overtones of N.A., which I know is a big issue for you," Eric offers.

"I'd love to go to that," I agree and Eric offers me a flyer for the next meeting.

Thane

I crawl into bed after a hectic shift and grab my phone. It's quarter to seven which means Madden should be calling any minute. We haven't hung out since pizza night, which was three weeks ago. However, we now have a standing phone date every other night at seven.

My phone rings and I spring to answer it, and then put on a casual tone.

"Hey."

"Hey, how was your day?" Madden asks.

"Not too bad. Kind of busy, luckily nothing too serious. What about you?"

"It was great." His voice lights up and I nestle down into my bed and wrap my arms around one of my pillows, closing my eyes and pretending he's right beside me instead of across town. "I signed up to teach a painting class at the park district, and all of my pieces at the consignment shop sold out."

"That's awesome baby, I'm so proud of you." I smile to myself, remembering the terrified broken man I fell in love with. He's so strong and capable now, and fuck if I don't love him even more.

On the other end of the line Madden clears his throat and I hear a rustling sound like he's re-adjusting his grip.

"So...uh...I was wondering...um...what are you doing Friday?" My heart gives a little squeeze as he stutters over his words.

"Nothing. Why, you want to hang out?"

"No, I want to take you on a date."

My mouth falls open as I replay his words in my head, making sure I didn't mishear them.

"You want to take me on a date?"

"Yes. I want to pick you up and take you out to dinner." He's more confident now, and my dick starts to harden. *I like this side of Madden.*

"I'd like that."

He lets out a relieved breath and I chuckle.

"Okay, awesome. Wear something sexy."

"Yes, sir," I tease.

"Alright, I'm going to let you go because I want to get a few more paintings done to take to the consignment shop. I'll pick you up at seven on Friday."

"Looking forward to it." I bite my tongue against saying 'I love you'. This feels like we're trying to make a new beginning and the last thing I want to do is push too far too fast.

Madden

I check my reflection one last time and run my hands through my moussed hair to give it a bit of a 'just fucked' look. And then, in lieu of my affirmations I do my best Buffalo Bill impression.

"Would you fuck me? Because I'd fuck me." I make a kissy face at my reflection and laugh. "Okay Madden, you've got this. You are stronger than you've ever been. You're killing this adulting thing. You are fucking awesome."

I pull into Thane's driveway twenty

minutes later and take a deep breath. I've already fucked and been fucked by this man, so why am I so nervous to take him out on a date? It's because this is our fresh start as well as a test for me. I've been doing so well, but there is a chance I'll have a panic attack in the restaurant, and if I do I need to get myself under control rather than letting Thane be the one to comfort me. That will no doubt, be a challenge for both of us.

Getting out of my car, I make my way to his door and knock. Thane answers after a few seconds, looking handsome as hell in a black button-up shirt and a pair of dark wash jeans.

"Hey."

"Hey."

Awkward greeting, check. Yep, this is definitely a first date.

I hold my hand out and Thane slips his fingers around mine. I tug him forward for a brief peck on the lips before tugging him toward my car before I say fuck dinner and push him back inside to have my way with him.

In the car on the way to the restaurant, we hold hands over the center console and talk about our week. I relax into the familiarity of being with Thane. It's hard to believe that all told I've known him about four months. It feels like a lifetime.

My paintings have been selling better than I expected. With a little padding in my bank account I decided to take Thane to a nice steakhouse downtown. When we get there I jump out of the car and run around to open his door for him.

"Wow, I'm getting the full treatment tonight."

"What can I say? I'm a gentleman." I say before pinching his ass.

I'm proud of myself as we enter the restaurant and my heartrate and breathing remains normal. I'm slightly tense, but not devolving into a panic attack. Thane glances at me and seems surprised to find that I'm smiling and standing tall, not crying in the corner.

I take Thane's hand again and lead him up to the hostess to give her my name. Since I made a reservation, we're taken straight back to a table.

"This place is really nice." Thane marvels, smoothing the white table cloth and glancing around like he's a little kid about to be caught with his hand in the cookie jar.

"Well, I had to impress my sexy date."

Thane's eyes soften.

"You don't have to impress me."

"Maybe I *want* to impress you."

Thane gives me a shy smile and my stomach flutters. Seconds later, the pop of a wine bottle being opened sounds and my body tenses. My brain kicks *into oh shit, we're going to die* mode.

My heartrate skyrockets and my muscles clench tight as I try to breathe. Thane makes a move toward me, but I manage to wave him off. He looks wary, but remains in his seat as I take a deep breath and hold it. I count to ten, and then let the breath out slowly. I repeat it, this time counting backward. After three slow breaths my heart starts to calm. I glance back up at Thane and give him a reassuring nod.

"I'm okay."

Thane's mouth is hanging open as he regards me with surprise and, dare I say, pride.

The rest of the meal goes off without a hitch as we fall into comfortable conversation about everything and nothing.

Thane

Madden's like a whole new man. The confidence I'd noticed over the phone is nothing compared to the man before me. The way he worked through his panic attack, the way he flirts with me throughout dinner like he doesn't have a care in the world. I'm hard as fuck and about ready to beg him to let me come home with him.

Madden seems to have different ideas as he orders us a dessert to share and lingers over a bottle of wine. Not that I'm complaining. Anywhere I can be with Madden is heaven on earth as far as I'm concerned.

By the time we're finished and back in Madden's car, I'm trying to think up a way to invite myself over to his place, or him to mine, without rushing things.

"Want to come back to my place for a cup of coffee?" Madden asks. *Fuck yeah!*

"Uh, sure." I play it off like I'm totally indifferent, while inside my head I'm rocking out to Christina Aguilera's *Dirrty*.

When we enter Madden's apartment, it's a whole different place than the last time I was here. He's got furniture and plants, there are even throw pillows.

"It looks great in here."

"Thanks. It's still small, but it feels more homey now." Madden makes his way to the kitchen and starts to make coffee. *What the hell? Since when does coffee actually mean coffee?*

He yawns as he measures out the coffee grounds.

"How've you been sleeping?"

"Good most nights. Other nights, not so good." He shrugs and then takes my hand and leads me to the couch where he guides my arm over his shoulder and snuggles against me.

God I've been missing the feeling of Madden against me these past few weeks. I nuzzle his neck and inhale until my lungs are nearly full to bursting with Madden's essence.

"Mmmm," he murmurs and burrows closer to me. As I caress his arm and hold him close, his eyes droop closed and his breathing deepens.

"Want me to go so you can get some sleep, baby?" I ask.

"Nuh-uh, stay." Madden pries his eyes open and stands from the couch. "Come on, let's go to bed."

I make a stop in the kitchen to turn off the

coffee maker and then follow Madden into the bedroom. His clothes are in a pile on the floor and I let mine join them, before climbing into bed beside him. Wrapping my arms around Madden, I pull him against my chest and breathe easy for the first time in almost a month.

I have no idea what time it is when I wake up with a warm body wrapped around me, but it's still dark out. Madden shifts against me in his sleep and his long, thick cock rubs against my ass. I try to stifle my moan, but it's been so fucking long. Unable to help myself I grind back against him and he murmurs sleepily. Madden's arms tighten around me and his fingers trail along my stomach and then into my boxers. Even half-asleep he's a fucking tease, tracing his fingers along my hips and thighs until I'm ready to promise him anything if he'll just touch my dick. I push back against his erection again and he whimpers. He fumbles to push my boxers down and then his own. I spit on my hand and reach back to use it to lube him up before positioning his length between my thighs. Madden moans again and kisses my shoulder as he starts to thrust between my legs.

The head of his cock glides against my balls sending jolts of pleasure up my spine. Madden's hand wraps around my aching erection and strokes me.

"Fuck, Madden," I moan into my pillow as his thrusts speed up, as does his hand.

"God, so good." Madden moans against my back.

My head falls back onto his shoulder and his lips ravage my neck, my jaw, any skin he can reach. Madden's body quivers and tenses against me before he lets out a loud groan and his cock begins to pulse against my balls, coating my thighs with his sticky cum. Even through his orgasm, he continues to pump my dick until I'm incoherent with pleasure.

When we're both spent we roll onto our backs and I turn my head to brush a kiss to Madden's lips. I should get up and clean myself up, but I'm too tired and relaxed now.

"I love you," Madden murmurs and then yawns.

"I love you too, baby." I kiss him one more time before I drift back off to sleep.

Madden

I wake up happier than I've been in weeks. I'm also sticky and annoyingly alone in bed. I grumble as I grab my boxers from where they are tangled in the sheets and pull them on. Then I go in search of the man who's supposed to be in my bed.

I don't have to look far, Thane is standing naked in my kitchen, making breakfast.

"I hope you're not frying bacon. I'd hate for you to get grease burns on that gorgeous cock."

"Just eggs, no risk to any of my glorious bits," he assures me, glancing over his shoulder and letting his eyes roam over my body.

I walk up behind him and wrap my arms around his middle, kissing the shell of his ear and then down the back of his neck.

"Can we talk real quick?"

My heart jumps into my throat. *Shit, did I mess this up before we could even get started?*

Thane nods towards the kitchen table and I take a seat.

"Last night...it feels like we're on the road to getting back together?" He says, sitting down across from me at the table.

I swallow and bob my head up and down, afraid to say anything.

"Okay, good. I want this to work out, I'm all in this and I want you to know that. That being said, I have to tell you that it was total bullshit the way you took off." I open my mouth to protest, defend myself, but he puts his hand up to stop me. "I understand why you did it, and agree it was the best thing for you at the time. I just want you to know that while I forgive you, I am pissed that it happened. If you ever pull that shit again, I'm not sure I'll be able to forgive it a second time."

"Understood."

"Good, now come over here and kiss me."

I scramble into his lap, not needing to be told twice. I kiss him with every ounce of longing I've bottled up inside me for the past three weeks.

"Oh shit, the eggs," Thane pulls away and I go back to my own chair while he tries to rescue breakfast. I watch his hot, bare ass as the muscles flex and twitch with every moment. *There's no way I'm ever giving this man up again.*

"By the way, I don't know how slow we're taking things, but my parents are coming for a visit next week. Would you maybe want to meet them?"

I tense and bite my bottom lip.

"I'm not so great with parents."

Thane returns to the table with two plates of eggs, sliding one in front of me.

"My parents are great. And they've been dying to meet my boyfriend ever since I came out to them." Thane hits me with puppy dog eyes and I can't say no.

"Ugh, fine," I groan, trying not to get too excited about the 'boyfriend' comment.

"Can we Netflix and Chill all day?"

"Hell yes."

Thane

I was nervous about having that talk with Madden first thing this morning. When I'd woken up for the second time, this time after the sun had come up, I laid there stroking his hair while he slept soundly. I re-memorized the feeling of his body in my arms, his breath against my neck, the way he murmurs in his sleep. This was the first time we'd slept in the same bed and he hadn't had a nightmare at some point during the night.

I'm in so much awe of how far he's come. I realize that Madden will likely always struggle with demons, not only from that night but from his childhood and his years on the streets. That's what makes him a beautiful person. Beauty is in the imperfections, it's what makes something real. And fuck if Madden isn't the realest person I've ever met.

I knew then that I'd have to clear the air about my feelings on the way he left, and the sooner the better. I wasn't going to let old hurt feelings poison our fresh start.

So, I'd gotten up and started cooking breakfast, mulling over how to bring up my feelings without Madden feeling attacked. When Madden woke up, it turned out to be easier than I'd expected and before I knew it the matter was settled and we were snuggling onto the couch in only our boxers, queuing up *Sons of Anarchy*.

"Want to know a secret?"

"Sure," Madden says, tilting his head up on my shoulder to look at me.

"I think you're way hotter than Charlie Hunnam."

Madden laughs and kisses the side of my jaw.

"You're so full of shit."

"I am not," I protest, grabbing Madden around the waist and hauling him onto my lap. "I bet you suck dick better than he does too."

"That's because he's so beautiful he never

has to suck dick, people line up to suck his."

"If that's your way of trying to get out of ever blowing me again…"

"Hell no, I love your big cock in my mouth." Madden grabs my erection through my boxers and strokes. "In fact…"

He drops to his knees and proves his point with enthusiasm.

And that's how we spent our first day back together, watching Netflix and taking turns making each other cum until our balls were empty and sore. Best. Day. Ever.

CHAPTER 17

Thane

"I don't think I can do this," Madden says. The expression on his face looks like he's about to hurl or make a run for it.

"Baby, this isn't a firing squad, it's my parents." I take his hand and kiss each knuckle and then give it a little squeeze of reassurance.

"Given the choice, I'd take the firing squad."

My heart aches for him, having nothing but negative and painful association with parental figures. My parents are going to love him, I know it.

Over the past month I'd made an effort to call my mom more often to check in and talk. I'd failed to mention to her that Madden and I were broken up. Call it wishful thinking. So, when they planned their visit she asked repeatedly if they would get to meet my boyfriend. She was over the moon about the idea. I was trying to think up a way to tell her that we weren't together at the moment when Madden had asked me on that date. So, I dodged that bullet.

I spot my parents stepping out of the airport and give Madden's hand one more squeeze before dropping it and rushing over to take their bags for them.

"Every time I see you it seems like you've put on more muscle," my mother accuses.

"Gotta be in shape to rescue cats from trees," I joke, giving her a kiss on the cheek and then turning to my dad for a hug.

"Oh, is that your boyfriend?" my mother whispers conspiratorially as she notices Madden leaning up against my car.

"Yeah, that's Madden," I confirm with a proud smile.

"He's a handsome one, isn't he?"

The laugh that escapes from me is part amusement, part relief. I can't believe it's this easy. Why the hell did I wait almost thirty years to tell them?

"Yes, he is," I agree with her.

As we approach, I notice Madden stiffen momentarily before giving my parents a forced smile.

"Madden, I'm so glad to meet you!" My mom exclaims, bypassing the hand Madden is holding out for a handshake and pulling him in for a bone-crushing hug instead.

"Um...hi...good to meet you Mrs..."

"Don't you dare call me anything so formal. You can call me Barbara or mom," she insists, causing Madden's face to flush deep red.

"Okay, Barbara, it's nice to meet you." Madden turns to my dad and offers his hand.

"Bob is fine, son. It's nice to meet you." My dad shakes his hand and pride fills my chest. I couldn't love my parents more in this moment.

"Alright, let's go home," I suggest, tossing their bags into my trunk and then opening the door for my mom and helping her into the car.

As soon as I'm in the driver's seat I reach across the center console and link my fingers with Madden. He seems a little less tense than a few minutes ago but is still strung pretty tight. I have no doubt he'll realize within the next few hours that he has nothing to fear from my parents.

Madden

After dinner Thane's mom spots *Cards Against Humanity* on Thane's bookshelf and gets very excited at the idea of playing. Thane became adorably flustered and tried to come up with a reason why we couldn't, even suggesting several other games. But Mrs... Barbara, wouldn't be deterred. So, here I am, meeting my boyfriend's parents for the first time and hearing his mother say the phrase "the taint, the grundle, the fleshy funbridge" and laughing so hard I'm worried I might cause myself internal damage.

"What's this mean?" His mom asks as she draws a new card.

"Kill me now," Thane mutters into his hands as his mother shows me the card in question. I choke on another laugh as I read the phrase 'road head' on her card.

"It's...um...well..."

"It's when you give a blowjob to a person

who's driving a car," Bob jumps in to answer.

"Oh, I didn't know *that's* what it was called." And then Bob grinned lecherously and I almost died in hysterics.

"Alright, we're done here." Thane snatches all the cards away from his parents while I try my damndest to breathe through my laughing fit.

By the time Thane has convinced his parents it's time for bed, I've gotten my laughing fit under control and am washing dishes while he makes sure they have everything they need in the guest bedroom.

Strong arms wrap around my waist as I dry the last of the plates and I relax back against my man.

"Stay the night," Thane murmurs against my shoulder.

"Wouldn't that be weird with your parents here?"

"I'm thirty-years-old, I think they might have guessed I've had sleepovers with my boyfriend."

I wrinkle my nose, not wanting his parents to have any idea of what we might get up to when we're alone. On the other hand, I'm loathe to go home to an empty bed.

"Alright, I'll stay."

I place the plate in the drying rack and turn around, place a small kiss on the tip of Thane's nose, and then take his hand and let him lead me upstairs to his bedroom.

The nightmares and insomnia have decreased considerably, but they're not gone. It's a little bit of déjà vu as I find myself watching *Golden Girls* at three in the morning on Thane's couch. I don't feel the hopeless, gnawing fear I used to feel, so it's an improvement.

I jump at the sound of footsteps behind me, turning around to find Thane's mom standing in the entrance to the living room, looking surprisingly awake for three in the morning.

"I'm sorry, did I wake you?"

"Oh no, I've had trouble sleeping my whole life," she waves me off and comes to sit on the couch beside me. "Oh, *Golden Girls.* I love this show."

"Me too," I agree.

We sit in companionable silence for a while before I have to ask.

"You *really* don't care that your son is gay?" I blurt. I realize not all parents are like mine, but my experience has been that at best most parents will have uncomfortable, grudging acceptance.

"Of course not, why would we?" Barbara seems surprised and offended that I'd even ask.

"Well, I'm sure you were hoping he'd marry a nice girl and give you a bunch of grandkids. Now all the sudden he's having you meet his boyfriend. That has to be a shock."

"It was a surprise," she concedes. "But we only care that Thane is happy. Although, I'd still love grandkids." She elbows me suggestively and we both laugh.

"Maybe one day." She smiles at my wistful tone and we fall back into comfortable silence, punctuated by laughter as we watch the show.

Thane

I wake up to find Madden and my mom cooking breakfast together. The scene gives me all sorts of squishy feelings as I watch them trade cooking tips and laugh together. My dad joins us as Madden is telling my mom about Rainbow House and how he does art with the kids there.

"Those poor kids, I can't believe anyone would throw their child out like that." My mom shakes her head at the thought of it. "We should find a place like that to volunteer," she says to my dad.

He nods in agreement as he sips his coffee.

"So, do you guys have anything specific you'd like to do today?" I always ask, because most of the time my parents come here with their own personal itinerary and I follow along.

"Madden said he wants to take us to see-"

"Shh," Madden cuts her off.

I raise an eyebrow and look between the two of them.

"It's a surprise," Madden explains.

"A surprise you told my mom about?"

"Yeah. We've been up together watching *Golden Girls* for hours. We got to talking," he explains with a shrug. "I want *you* to be surprised."

"Alright," I agree.

After breakfast and showers, we're piled into Madden's car headed to our undisclosed location. As scenery passes, I try to make guesses about where Madden might be taking us, but each time he laughs and shakes his head no.

Twenty minutes into the drive he exits the highway near the nightclub. I glance at Madden out of the corner of my eye to check his reaction. Does he realize we're so close? Are we going to drive right by it?

I'm even more surprised as he continues to make all the turns that will take us to the club. He isn't even flinching as he puts on his blinker directly in front of the parking lot and turns in.

"What are we doing here?"

"It's what I have to show you."

"Are you okay?" I watch him closely for any signs of distress.

Madden laughs as he puts the car in park.

"I'm fine. To be honest, I had a pretty bad panic attack the first day I came back," Madden says.

"*The first day?* You've been coming here a lot?"

"Yeah, come on, I'll show you." Madden takes my hand and pulls me around the side of the building, my parents not far behind. As soon as we're around the corner, I see it. My mouth falls open as I take it in.

"It's amazing. You did all this?" I take a step back to admire all of it. The entire side of the building is painted with a mural. There are hearts, rainbows, and images of all different kinds of couples locked in embraces. In big, bubble letters at the bottom it says '#loveisthecure'.

"I had some help," Madden admits.

"Who?"

"The guys, of course. And a bunch of kids from Rainbow House. About three weeks ago I decided to contact the owner of the club about the idea. He loved it, so I got everyone together and we created beauty to replace the pain."

"This is amazing," I say again.

"I'm glad you're never on social media, it would've ruined the surprise because this is going crazy viral."

I whip out my phone and sure enough #loveisthecure is trending with thousands of people across the country sharing images of the mural and talking about making their own in their towns.

"You are the most incredible man I've ever known."

Madden blushes and rolls his eyes to deflect the compliment, but I can tell it means something to him.

My parents gush over the mural as well until we all decide on our next activity, walking around downtown.

With Madden's hand in mine, it feels like everything is right in the universe.

CHAPTER 18

Thane

"You sure you're up for this, baby?" I ask, as Madden stands in my bathroom moussing his hair.

"Absolutely. Please, don't coddle me. If I freak out, I'll deal with it, but I need to do this. My therapist agrees that it'll be good for me to face my biggest hurdle surrounded by all my friends."

I sigh but nod to show I'm in agreement. I hate the idea of Madden suffering. Since getting back together, I've had to learn to reign in my protective streak. Not entirely, Madden still lets me take care of him sometimes. We had a few sessions with his therapist together so I could understand how to be supportive without making Madden feel like I was coddling him or not letting him support himself. It helped a lot, but it's a learning process for both of us.

"Stop looking so glum, we're going to have fun," Madden says, turning me and pushing me toward my closet to pick out something to wear.

I grab a pair of worn jeans that hug my ass in a way that drives Madden crazy, and tug a black t-shirt over my head. Foregoing the primping and hair styling that Madden does, I'm ready to go in under five minutes.

We pull up in front of the bar down the street from Heathens Ink, where Madden told everyone we'd meet them tonight. I glance at Madden out of the corner of my eye, checking for any signs of distress. He's a little tense, but it seems more on the borderline of excitement rather than anxiety.

Madden glances over and gives me a reassuring smile and a kiss on the cheek.

"You worry too much, I'm going to be fine."

As soon as I have the car in park Madden is out the door, bouncing on his toes for me to hurry up.

"Come on, before I lose my nerve," he jokes, waving his hands in a 'hurry up' motion.

When we get inside, I let Madden know I'm going to stop at the restroom real quick and ask if he'll be okay. He waves me off with more reassurances and heads toward the bar top.

After I use the bathroom, I go in search of Madden and when I find him, I'm hit with a sense of déjà vu. He's leaning over the bar, smiling at the bartender, looking all kinds of sexy and confident. It hits me like a lightning bolt to the chest, how far we've come in such a short time. I can't imagine my life without Madden in it.

I approach him as the bartender is sliding

his drink over, with a phone number written on the napkin beneath.

"Let me get that for you." I hand the bartender a ten and Madden smiles at me before straightening up and offering me his hand.

"Madden," he plays along, offering me his name.

"It's *very* nice to meet you Madden. Are you here alone?"

"I came with my boyfriend, but he seems to have disappeared and what he doesn't know won't hurt him."

"You're bad," I accuse, stepping close and sneaking a hand under the hem of his shirt, around his waist.

"Get a room," Zade's teasing call pulls us out of our game and Madden laughs.

"I guess we *did* come here to socialize," he laments. "We're going to need to explore some stranger roleplay in the near future."

"Agreed."

We make our way over to the crowded table where all of our friends are waiting for us.

Madden

I'm doing it. I'm actually fucking doing it. I'm standing in a bar, with my friends, and I'm not freaking out. Sure, I'm a little tense, but it's nothing a few more drinks won't solve. I can't wait to tell Eric how I did. He wasn't sure I was ready for this step. But I knew, I could feel it.

Everything is perfect. I've got my friends, my boyfriend, and best of all I have my life back. Granted, it's not the same life I had. I flex my hand instinctively. It doesn't hurt and my muscles are strong, but it still remains to be seen if the nerve damage will repair itself. I may or may not ever tattoo again. At least I still have my painting, the classes I'm teaching, Rainbow House. I have a whole life. And, it's a damn good life.

I can't stop myself from grabbing Thane by the back of the neck and dragging him into a deep, hungry kiss. I didn't think it was possible to love someone this much.

When I finally let him pull away, there's a smile on his damp, kiss swollen lips.

"I love you," I say before giving him one more peck on the lips.

"I love you, too."

"If you guys are going to suck each other's faces off all night then go home now," Adam razzes us.

"No more face sucking, I promise," I assure him with a laugh.

"Good, I'd hate to make you leave when this is the first time you've made it here in months."

"Yeah, I've missed our Friday nights here."

Adam puts an arm around my shoulder and gives me a squeeze.

"Alright, who's buying the next round?" Adam asks and all of us quickly touch our noses. I glance over at Thane who's looking confused and then chagrined.

"Hope you fuckers don't expect to nail me on that more than once," he warns but heads to the bar to get everyone's drinks.

"He's a keeper," Royal says as Thane stalks away.

"That he is," I agree.

As the night goes on it's impossible to miss the way Zade brushes casual touches against Royal's skin at every opportunity. Each time Royal shivers and smiles, looking like a man utterly smitten. I'm right in the middle of giving myself a pat on the back for pushing those two together when I notice Nash. He's watching Royal and Zade's interaction, too. Instead of looking happy for his best friend, he looks...jealous? Forlorn? *Fuck*.

"Is it just me or is Nash looking at Royal in kind of a...well...gay way?" I whisper to Thane. He discreetly glances towards Nash and then to Royal and Zade a few bar stools down from us.

"Yeah, he looks like he wants a taste," Thane agrees.

"Damnit. I hope to hell this doesn't turn into love triangle bullshit, I *hate* love triangles. You never know who you're supposed to root for. Or, if you do pick a team, that's always the one who gets dumped."

"I wouldn't worry too much about it. Between you and me, Zade is polyamorous so if it's up to him he'll find a way to make it work for the three of them."

"Polyamorous? Like he prefers open relationships?" I ask, curious.

"No, he likes committed, exclusive relationships between three or more men," Thane clarifies.

"So, did the two of you have other...boyfriends?" I ask, almost not wanting to know the answer. The idea of Thane in some big sweaty orgy doesn't sit well.

Thane barks out a laugh.

"God no, monogamy all the way for me. Zade just told me once that in his perfect future he'd have two partners. He said he has too much love to give."

"I'm sure it's going to be interesting watching those three navigate that relationship, then."

"No doubt," Thane agrees.

It's not long before Gage sidles up beside me, looking me up and down like he's checking to make sure I'm holding it together. Even though I've lived with Gage for four years, I've never been as close to him as I have with Royal and Adam. If I had to guess I'd say it's because Gage is sort of the strong silent type. He's always been nice, but I always got the impression he wasn't looking to get close to me. In fact, Adam is about the only person he is close to and they've been best friends since childhood. From my understanding, Gage took it hard when Adam's brother committed suicide six years ago...*and now I understand why he's looking at me so weird.*

"I'm okay," I assure him.

"You sure?" he brings his bottle of beer to his lips, not breaking eye contact.

"I'm positive. I've never been better."

Gage holds my gaze for another several seconds before finally nodding and looking away. His attention seems to land on Adam who, instead of making the rounds in the bar and hitting on women, is sitting on his phone.

"He told you what's been going on with him lately?" Gage asks me, nodding towards Adam to indicate who he's referring to.

"No."

"He's been...off lately. Kira hasn't been coming around."

"That's not a bad thing," I point out. Gage hates Kira as much as I do. It's difficult not to hate Kira, she's a right cunt.

"No it's not," Gage agrees with a chuckle. "I get the feeling there's something he's not telling me. He's been distant, closed off. Sometimes I get the feeling like he's about to say something, then he shakes his head and leaves the room. Now he's got some new online girlfriend or *something*. He's constantly on his phone but he won't tell me anything about who he's talking to. I don't understand what's up with him."

"I'm sure if it's anything important he'll tell you."

"Johnny didn't." Gage says. I've never heard

him mention Adam's brother before and it takes me a second to realize that's who he means. "You didn't."

"Gage, man, Adam's not suicidal," I do my best to reassure him. He shakes his head and huffs out a breath.

"It's hard to tell. You never know for sure," Gage argues.

"He's your best friend, why don't you try talking to him? Even if he's not ready to tell you, at least he'll know you're there to listen when he is ready."

Gage nods and finishes the last of his beer before walking away.

"Having fun?" Thane asks once we're alone again.

"Yeah, but I'm ready to go home." I slip a finger into his belt loop and tug him forward. "I'm kind of dying to suck my boyfriend's cock."

"Well, there's no way I'm going to argue with that." Thane nips at my bottom lip before taking my half-empty drink out of my hand, setting it down, and starts dragging me toward the door. I manage to wave goodbye to the guys over my shoulder as we go.

As soon as the door to my apartment is closed I shove Thane up against it and drop to my knees. I press my nose against the prominent bulge in his jeans and grab his hips.

"God I love your cock. And I need it in my mouth, now."

I start tearing at his button fly, desperate to taste him. Thane moans, running his fingers through my hair. His head hits the door with a soft thud as I lick along his happy trail while I get his pants off.

I don't waste any time. The moment his pants are around his ankles, his dick is deep in my mouth.

"Fuck, Madden," Thane gasps.

What this blowjob lacks in finesse it more than makes up for in enthusiasm as I slobber and suck like my life depends on it. Reaching between his legs I cup Thane's balls, giving them a gentle squeeze then rolling them around in my palm.

"God, baby, so good... fuck, I'm close," Thane warns and I relax my throat to take his cock deeper. When the ring of my throat constricts around his glans Thane cries out, his whole body tensing.

I suck him until he stops pulsing deep in my throat and when I pull off, he sags against the door.

"You're the best boyfriend ever."

"I know," I say with a cheeky smile, pulling his underwear back into place and holding him steady as he steps out of his pants. "Just leave those by the door, we'll get them later."

Thane doesn't argue, just follows me to the bedroom, losing his shirt somewhere along the way as well.

I strip down to my boxers and climb into bed, letting Thane pull me close and wrap his arms around me.

"Sometimes I wish I hadn't gone to the bar that night. But then I realize I never would've met you. So, it was kind of a tradeoff. You know?"

"Yeah." Thane's eyes roam over my face as he brings his hand up and cups my jaw, running his thumb along the stubble of my day-old beard growth. "What do you think would've happened if there hadn't been a shooting? If we'd just gone back to my place and had sex all night, do you think we'd still be *here* now?"

"Without a doubt. This is where we're meant to be. And all the bumps and bruises along the way were well worth it."

Thane squeezes me tighter and kisses all over my face until I'm laughing and squirming in his arms.

"I want you to make love to me." I start stripping off my boxers before he even answers.

"As if you even have to ask."

EPILOGUE

6 month later
Madden

"Are you sure about this?" I ask as Thane relaxes into my tattoo chair and I try to remember how to set up to do a damn tat.

"Of course I'm sure, I want your mark on my body," Thane purrs. Fuck, when he puts it that way...

"What if I fuck up? My hand doesn't shake much anymore, but what if..."

"Shh," Thane leans forward and covers my mouth to stop me from talking. "It's going to be great. Now give me some ink."

"Fine, but don't blame me if it turns out looking like garbage."

Thane rolls his eyes and settles back again, seemingly unconcerned.

I'd come to live with the idea that I'd likely never tattoo again. I'd managed to make a decent living over the past six months selling paintings and teaching art classes at the park district. I even set up my own Etsy page to sell my work and it's been selling faster than I can paint it. Little by little, the shake in my hand diminished until it was almost gone. I've been terrified to actually get back up on the horse so the speak, though. Then, this morning, Thane woke me up with a blow-job. When I was weak, vulnerable, and would've agreed to anything, he asked me to tattoo him today.

So, here we are. In my work space at Heathens Ink for the first time in nearly a year while I setup my equipment.

In spite of my nerves it feels so right to be back in my space. I'm sure it'll be like riding a bike, right?

I pop a mint into my mouth, because it's what I always do when I'm inking, and I pull on a pair of gloves.

"Let's do this," I crack my neck and roll my stool forward. As soon as the needle touches his skin I feel at one with the universe once again.

"Hey, Madden," Thane says, pulling me out of my own head. I glance up at him and he's gazing at me with admiration. "Marry me?"

My finger slips off the button and I pull the tattoo gun back so I don't fuck up. My hands are shaking so bad there's no way I can keep going right now.

"What?" I'm sure I misheard him over the buzzing of the needle. There's no way he asked me out of the blue to marry him, is there?

"Marry me," he says again, clear as day, with a big ass grin on his face.

"Fuck yeah." I launch myself into his lap and

kiss the hell out of him.

The End

MORE BY K.M.NEUHOLD

The Heathens Ink Series

➢ Rescue Me (Heathens Ink, 1). To read this story about dealing with PTSD and addiction, and finding true love during an inconvenient time: click here

➢ Going Commando (Heathens Ink,2). If you're looking for a lower angst story, you'll want to check out this sexy, fun friends-to-lovers with an epic twist! Get it Here

➢ From Ashes (Heathens Ink, 3). Don't miss this story about love in the face of deep physical and emotional scars: Click Here

➢ Shattered Pieces (Heathens Ink, 4). Grab this beautiful story about a feisty man who loves to wear lace and makeup trying his damndest to help a wounded soul heal: Click Here

➢ Inked in Vegas (Heathens Ink, 5) Join the whole crew for some fun in Las Vegas! Click HERE

➢ Flash Me (Heathens Ink, 6) Liam finally gets his men! Click HERE

The Heathens Ink Spin-off Series: Inked

➢ Unraveled (Inked, 1) And don't forget to read

the sexy, kinky friends to lovers tale! Click Here

➢ Uncomplicated (Inked, 2) Beau, the flirty bartender finally gets his HEA!

Replay Series

➢ If you missed the FREE prequel to the Replay series, get to know the rest of the band better! Click Here

➢ Face the Music (Replay, 1): click Here

➢ Play it by Ear (Replay, 2): click Here

➢ Beat of Their Own Drum (Replay, 3): Click Here

Ballsy Boys

Love porn stars? Check out the epic collaboration between K.M. and Nora Phoenix! Get a free prequel to their brand new series, and the first two books now!

➢ Ballsy (A Ballsy Boys Prequel). Meet the men who work at the hottest gay porn studio in L.A. in this FREE prequel! Click Here

➢ Rebel (Ballsy Boys, 1) If anyone can keep it casual it's a porn star and a break-up artist. Right?? Click Here

➢ Tank (Ballsy Boys, 2) Don't miss this enemies to lovers romance that will set your Kindle on fire! Click Here

➢ Heart (Ballsy Boys, 3) Like a little ménage action with your porn stars? Don't miss bad boy porn star Heart falling for not only his nerdy best friend, Mason, but also his own parole officer, Lucky! Click Here

➢ Campy (Ballsy Boys, 4) a sexy cowboy and a porn star with secrets! Grab Campy's story now! Click Here

Working Out the Kinks

➤ Stay (Working Out The Kinks, 1) What happens to a couple when one of them discovers a kink he's not so sure his partner will be into? Enjoy this super cute, low-angst puppy play story! Click Here

Stand-Alone Shorts

➤ Always You- A super steamy best friends to lovers short! A post-college weekend, a leaky ceiling, and a kiss they weren't expecting. Click Here

➤ That One Summer- A Young Adult story about first love and the one summer that changes everything. Click Here

➤ Kiss and Run- A 30k steamy, Valentine's Day novella. Click Here

ABOUT THE AUTHOR

Author K.M.Neuhold is a complete romance junkie, a total sap in every way. She started her journey as an author in new adult, MF romance, but after a chance reading of an MM book she was completely hooked on everything about lovely- and sometimes damaged- men finding their Happily Ever After together. She has a strong passion for writing characters with a lot of heart and soul, and a bit of humor as well. And she fully admits that her OCD tendencies of making sure every side character has a full backstory will likely always lead to every book having a spin-off or series. When she's not writing she's a lion tamer, an astronaut, and a superhero...just kidding, she's likely watching Netflix and snuggling with her husky while her amazing husband brings her coffee.

STALK ME

Website: authorkmneuhold.com
Email: kmneuhold@gmail.com
Instagram: @KMNeuhold
Twitter: @KMNeuhold
Bookbub
Join my Mailing List for special bonus scenes and teasers!
Facebook reader group- Neuhold's Nerds You want to be here, we have crazy amounts of fun

Made in United States
Orlando, FL
17 May 2022

17962504R00135